MARILOU IS EVERYWHERE

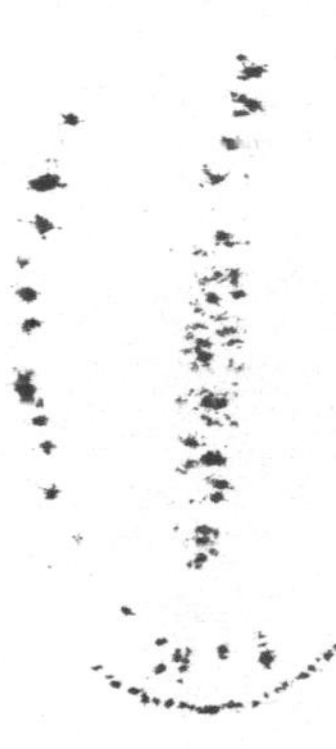

MARILOU IS EVERYWHERE

Sarah Elaine Smith

HAMISH HAMILTON
an imprint of
PENGUIN BOOKS

HAMISH HAMILTON

UK | USA | Canada | Ireland | Australia
India | New Zealand | South Africa

Hamish Hamilton is part of the Penguin Random House group of companies whose addresses can be found at global.penguinrandomhouse.com.

First published in the United States of America by Riverhead Books 2019
First published in Great Britain by Hamish Hamilton 2020
001

This is a work of fiction. Names, characters, places and incidents either are the product of the author's imagination or are used fictitiously, and any resemblance to actual persons, living or dead, business establishments, events or locales is entirely coincidental

Printed and bound in Great Britain by Clays Ltd, Elcograf S.p.A.

A CIP catalogue record for this book is available from the British Library

ISBN: 978-0-241-40094-4

www.greenpenguin.co.uk

MIX
Paper from responsible sources
FSC® C018179

Penguin Random House is committed to a sustainable future for our business, our readers and our planet. This book is made from Forest Stewardship Council® certified paper.

For Janice Hatfield

I used to think my troubles got legs the summer Jude Vanderjohn disappeared, but now I see how they started much earlier.

Before that summer, the things that happened to me were air and water and just as see-thru. They were real but I didn't care for them much. I did not care for the real. It didn't seem so special to me, whatever communion I could take with the dust spangles, or the snakes that spun in an oiled way along the rotting tractor tires stacked up by the shed, or the stony light that fell in those hills and made the vines and mosses this vivid nightmare green. None of it had a purpose to me. Everything I saw seemed to have been emptied out and left there humming. I watched the cars. I read catalogs, which I collected and which my family called Cindy's magazines. My life was an empty place. From where I stood, it seared on with a blank and merciless light. All dust and no song. Rainbows in oil puddles. Bug bites hatched with a curved X from my fingernails. Donald Duck orange juice in the can. Red mottles on my brother Clinton's puffy hands, otherwise so white they were actually yellow, like hard cheese. The mole on my belly button. You get to know things this way, by looking at yourself. You know the world by the shape of what comes back when you yell.

I had only ever been myself, and found it lacking. Even when the sun was shining, when the world was up, when I was born. And some days, I was really, really born. Most of my day I spent carving little pits in time where I could hide out in a texture of light or an idea. And then, that summer, I made a space between myself and all that. I guess how I could say it is, I began to see the other world, and it was not real and yet I could pull it across the real at will, like a thin cotton curtain. When I stood just far enough outside of it, my life, suddenly the blaring light resolved itself into a huge movie screen blooming out of the dark, a woman's jaw jutting into the abandoning tilt of a kiss. The beginning of romance came from that distance. Black and white, the sparkling velvet dark and always someone else is there in the mind, in the cavern above my head. But a stranger. But it doesn't matter, really. The point is that at that moment in my life, I would kill or die, die or kill, to be anyone else.

I wasn't trying to become Jude. Not exactly. But I wanted to disappear, and she had left a space. When I stepped into that space, I vanished from my senses. It changed me into someone who didn't have my actual mind. The same way it changed Jude, when Virgil called her Marilou as they walked the halls of our high school arm in arm, shining like magazine people you'd never see. She became that other girl, and it lit her up, and that is what I wanted.

Now, I know how that sounds: teenage, teenage. I was, and it brought me to wickedness. Except in wickedness, I loved the world, too, in a way so fierce I assumed no one could imagine. And I love it still. It was, quite simply, how I survived.

I

Jude Vanderjohn was last seen in the parking lot across from Burchinal's General Store in Gans, just over the West Virginia border, where she had been camping in Coopers Rock State Forest with four other girls from the newly graduated West Greene High School senior class. The quickest way back went through Morgantown, but they had gone instead through Fayette County. When asked why they took the long way, Kayla apparently said that they wanted a prettier drive, they weren't anxious to come back so soon. Then, when Detective Torboli asked again, she admitted they had wanted to smoke a blunt in the car, and Jude had a strict personal law against blunt smoking on interstates. Which did turn out to be true, but it wasn't the real reason either.

Eventually Crystal admitted that they had been followed, and took the other route because they were trying to lose the boys who had been hanging around their campsite. The boys had seemed vaguely related. They all had a similar smudge of mustache and they spoke in a brisk mystery language. At first, Shawn, B.D., and Caleb had loitered in a helpful way, starting the fire and sharing from their thirty racks, showing off places around the margins of Cheat Lake where the fish were so gullible you'd think they wanted to die in your hands.

The second night of the trip, the boys took them on a hike through some path that wound around the massive blocks of limestone stories below the lookout pavilion. They took secret avenues through the rock where slim light fell through, silvery and ancient. At the Ravens Rock Overlook, they had produced homemade blackberry wine in a three-liter Pepsi bottle. They were romance minded, of course. The girls didn't rebuff them too hard at first. It is sometimes nice to see a little attention. A little of that light lands on you, say, on a dizzy vista, and sweet wine is sweet, or so I'm told.

Thrill seekers prefer Ravens Rock Overlook because it is unfenced. The view isn't troubled by those coin-op lookie-loos. It feels likely, if you place a foot wrong, that you will spin off into the sky and never again trouble with gravity. So the boys dared to touch the girls in the dark, on the small of the back, the casual first declaration. It was romance. Apparently Kayla even held hands with Shawn, the tall one with the buff of his arms showing through his cut-up T-shirt. They talked about the souls of animals and the things the stars looked like, and they talked about their idiot worried parents and how they would all be just fine.

Shawn walked Kayla closer to the edge. He said he wanted to show her a place where you could see the river down below like a moving silver chain. Close to the drop, he kicked her in the back of the knee, sly, to make her stumble and grab on to him dearly. Kayla pantomimed this by pinwheeling her arms in dismay when she told me the story. Shawn had probably intended for her to swoon into his arms, but she instead shrieked and tore back up from the edge, and running blind in the dark she turned her ankle in a gopher hole. The boys carried her back to camp and bound her ankle with duct tape and even went to the Eagle Lodge Café to bring her ice, a Coke, a stack of cordwood to apologize.

But things had turned. Suddenly Kayla's absent boyfriend asserted himself a bit more firmly in her memory. She started to talk about him a lot. Maybe she was trying to remind herself as much as anything, but she did allude to Lyle's WPIAL wrestling trophies and bow-hunting expertise something on the heavy side. The musk wore down to a lean little smell. But the boys kept working their angle, saying how cold a night for

May. Saying, man, what a lonely thing, to sleep alone on a night so cold. When the girls didn't respond they laid it down for a while and kept up the friendliness, but Jude had already heard the sour note. She said she didn't like their manners and they could go bang their dicks together if they were so fucking cold. The smallest of the boys, B.D., feint-stepped to her with his hand rared back, like he would slap her in the face, and they noticed then that he had a knife. It was nothing special, with a black plastic handle like for a kitchen, but he let it wave around meanly all the same. Jude brought out a canister of pepper spray—none of the others knew she even carried such a thing—and scorched B.D. right at the bridge of his nose.

Tia and Crystal and Kayla wanted to leave immediately, but it had already been dark for some time and they had left the cars outside the park limits to avoid the vehicle fee. Jude and Amber doubted the boys would come back, and with Kayla on one foot it would take forever to hike out in the dark. But the boys did pass through a few times in the night to thrash around in the underbrush and scare them, muttering under their breath in a simmering way: *bitches, bitches, bitches*. Crystal was sure someone had peed on her tent in the middle of the night.

In the morning, they broke camp as soon as the light started to change and hiked back out of the park. Jude's car was scratched up with key marks that bit down to the metal. They had not told the boys where they'd left their cars, but Jude realized one must have followed her when she had made the trek to get bug spray from the trunk. Still, she didn't seem scared, they said. Pissed off, though, like anyone would be.

Once they were loaded up and driving off, a shitty Chevy Corsica pulled out of the brush by the highway entrance and kicked up hard behind them on the turns, swinging out into the oncoming lane and passing them on blind curves, then slowing down to nothing so the girls would have to go around. Amber, who was driving the other vehicle, claimed the Corsica nipped her rear bumper a few times, and though they brought it in to gather evidence, nothing could be discerned from the condition of her car. Jude, who was driving in front, pulled off toward Uniontown. She said she knew a back way. The boys didn't follow.

Jude's car was still in front. She didn't know her way so well as she thought—they were about to enter a toll road, and she swerved off at the last exit before the turnpike. Her vehicle was knocking and slugging to accelerate, and as they went through Gans, it slowed up and seemed to shake on the turns. On one hairpin she hit a pothole and limped it into the parking lot across from Burchinal's, where a hand-lettered sign advertised a pepperoni roll sale for the students of Ferd Swaney Elementary and the American flag hung rigid like it does everywhere. An old boy in greased coveralls and no undershirt was smoking in a watchful way on his porch, right up by the road, as they peeped the dark windows. Closed, Sunday morning, for church. He came out from behind a dismembered Honda Rebel to look at Jude's car. From what they described, he said it sounded like someone had put sugar in her gas tank and the fuel filter would have to be dumped. He offered his services, or she could use the phone inside to call AAA. Jude chose to call, even though it would take a few hours. She waved him off and called on her cell. She must have had it with friendly men by that point.

The other girls were getting anxious. They had a mutual friend who was getting married in Nineveh that afternoon, and while they didn't want to abandon Jude, it happened that Kayla, Crystal, Amber, and Tia were all in the wedding party, and Jude was not. Morgan, the bride, expected them at eleven to have their hair duded up with mini rhinestones and all that. More to the point, Morgan was a real grudge keeper and had already dis- and reinvited Amber multiple times, so they were relieved when Jude told them to go on. The old boy said Jude could wait inside the store. It just so happened to belong to his uncle. He fished a key out from the mailbox and let them into the unlit place already decided. He gave them Cokes to calm them down, and said he hoped they would all pass through again someday on happier errands.

It was not even clear whether he or his wife had been the last person to see Jude. His name was Denny Cogar and he advised that the tow truck arrived around two, many hours after it was supposed to come. He also advised that he had watched Jude hitch herself up into the cab and laugh with the driver about something. But Cheryl Cogar recalled that Jude had spent a long time on her cell phone, pacing along the crick behind the store, talking to someone, fighting, kind of, and hours before the tow truck arrived, she had gotten into a low little hat-shaped sedan that had skidded up from nowhere.

"And they was playing loud music about riding for the devil," Cheryl said. "Gangster music, I think it was."

"You saw Jude get into this car?"

"I heard it."

"What kind of car was it?" Detective Torboli asked.

"Red," she said.

"Nothing else?"

"It was red."

The interview pressed on along this line for hours. The detective named all types of cars in a soft, chanting voice.

II

The summer Jude disappeared, my brothers and I had turned basically feral since our mother had gone off for a number of months and we were living free, according to our own ideas and customs. Our mother disappearing was nothing new, but she usually came back within a few weeks. This time, we had not exactly been counting the days, but we had run out of food maybe a month past and been improvising ever since. I was fourteen and ruled by a dark planet. My brothers were grown, or seemed so to me at the time. In winter, they ate Steak-umms in front of the TV and made up theories about the New World Order while Clinton got lazy angry drunk around twilight. But in summer, Virgil lined up mowing jobs all over, and they were suddenly honest workingmen, and you couldn't tell them a single thing.

Our well was low from a dry spring, so we bathed in the pond. We called it Heaven Lake because we had grand imaginations and no sense, but it was really just a retainer pond. The family that owned it was called the Dukes and they had built a house, too, which looked like a blank face. They had made the pond, just scratched it right in and pulled the silver into it somehow with backhoes and a spillway of cinder blocks. They peopled it with catfish and bluegill. It was fenced in at the road with an eighteen-foot chain-link gate. The family kept it locked all the time except when they wanted to swim or fish, although they only came up a few times each year and the place was essentially ours.

We usually walked along our ridge and dropped down to it through the brambles and little saplings that gave way under our hands. It was harder to get over the fence. Once I'd gotten stuck at the top with a leg on either side, petrified of swinging the other leg over and losing my balance. Virgil got me down by shaking the fence with his fists. I didn't so much as smile at him for two weeks.

Clinton slid down the steep parts on his feet, going in long pulls, and caught himself on hemlocks to slow up. Virgil walked down steady with his feet slanted sideways, sometimes testing the branches and footholds before he dropped his weight down on them. Virgil wasn't scared of much, but he hated walking down steep places, especially if they were rocky and shifting. It always surprised me to see him look so careful. When he focused, it painted something hard and solemn over his eyes.

The pond looked alive to me, even the shape of the hills around it. I lit it up by looking at it. I had made its very image. I felt, all at the same moment, that it was valiant for beauty and also so plain that it embarrassed me to belong to it. On the steep tractor paths and under the hawthorns, fine dappled mushrooms winked like they had invented themselves, sporelike, and had materialized from the floaters in your eyes.

The good thing about washing up at the pond was we could also catch fish in it. I didn't ask anymore why we were going to do something. This made it easier, because then I just did the things that happened and each moment was like turning a page in a book and it felt easy to me. The shade was icy. Something in the air was touching on the cold water and carrying it in big bold rushes under the trees.

I couldn't remember how long she was gone, except there had still been snow when our mother left. I knew because I remembered the cold air shoving itself in while she stood in the doorway and gave Virgil a bank envelope. It was supposed to last us. There was a job, she said, and the money could last us a long time, but she had to be away to do it. She told Virgil how to go pay the light bill at the customer service counter at the grocery store in town. Her car was already running with the fumes sinking down and snaking and spreading. It had seemed like midnight but it was just after dinner.

Virgil carried the fishing poles. Clinton wasn't allowed to carry anything since he more or less let himself fall down the hill, just stopping before the last drop. He once had smashed the tackle box when his foot hit a mud skid that sent him tumbling down to a broad shelf held up by tree roots. All the lures and hooks went dazzle in the undergrass, shining so much I could hear them almost. I had to carry the tackle box since then.

Near the bottom, Clinton dropped out of sight. There was a wall of shale there. You could either pick around the side and come down to level slowly, or race off and fall the last six feet. Virgil and I wound around to the side. He put me in front and laid his huge hand on my skull.

"First thing, I want you to get in the water and wash up, OK?"

Virgil had put a bottle of shampoo in his back pocket before we left the house. I knew my hair was gummy under his hand. It stuck under my nose and on my cheeks with its oil. I couldn't smush the oil off with the back of my hand anymore because it was getting too thick.

Lately I felt funny about him touching me. I felt funny about all men. At school, I had punched Justin Deeba in the stomach when he said he liked me as we stood in the lunch line. I couldn't think what else to do. He dropped the confetti plastic tray. The gray green beans and their juice and blubs of salt pork got all down his shirt and down the front of his pants. My face had gotten so I thought it was melting, but I was crying. And I loved how it felt. I spent the rest of the day hiding in the woods behind school, trying to look into the white sky hard enough for it to shimmer.

Also, I had noticed that men smelled. They smelled like pepper and skunk and oil. Some reeked of it. It frightened me that lately this smell came off my brothers, too.

When we got to the water, Clinton was already in, ducking his head under and coming up with his mouth wide and his hair flat and bright across his shoulders. He walked out and took off his clothes and laid them out to bleach in the sun. He pulled on a bottle of pink muscat wine and spat some at Virgil.

"Fucking stop it," Virgil said.

"Fucking make me," Clinton said. He fell back again into the water, slapping home on it. Virgil got tense whenever anybody was drinking or getting stoned. He had never drunk a bit of alcohol. He tried not to make it a big deal, but once I saw him sip on Clinton's coffee cup by mistake and spit wine right on the floor, and go wash out his mouth over and over.

I had to do something about the snakes before I could get in the water. I found a few big rocks and carried them to the dock. I threw them down hard so they would send a tail of white water gutting up from the surface, one after another so the snakes would get scared off. This I had always done, since I was little. It was kind of a joke that I still did it, but not the kind of joke that made anyone laugh. Then I walked back around to the marshy edge where the water was shallow and warm and fine like dog hair and started getting in barefooted with my feet sucking down. I didn't like to jump in just yet. I liked the feel of the water coming up my legs and dimpling where my hairs stuck in it. I did it slow so I could get used to the cold.

Once Virgil was on the flat land, he jumped in from the dock to make himself look brave again. He and Clinton bashed each other's heads against the water and kicked. He put some of the shampoo over his shirt and ran his hands to suds it up, then dove down. But he got out again almost right away and laid his wet clothes where Clinton had, then put out the tackle box and started thinking through it.

The fishing spot was on the other side of the pond where it cut deep into the sycamore banks above it. I could just still see them casting out over there. Their reflections sent out flying tentacles that kissed up at the place where their hooks landed. Virgil was using my Snoopy rod, even though it was sized for a girl, since it brought him the best luck. He always asked me for permission to use it, even though he had given it to me for my eighth birthday.

Alone in the water I bladed my hand through it until my fingers got grainy. I hugged my legs and arms in to feel the sink. Around one end, benches ringed the dock. The boards were broad and flat so I could lie myself out full length on them and get my front half dry from the sun, all the sticky water shrinking while it dried up. It left a dust all over me. Something was wrong with my skin. When it got wet, I could rub on it to make gray strings, and then sweep them away. In my ankle hollows, the skin was hard and brown and I could peel it off with a fingernail. What was underneath was dusty and white.

Once I felt good and hot, like the muscles were about to fall off my bones, I would jump back in from the dock and feel the water shock me to pieces. I was getting a body. One day my mother had stopped me at the door and informed me in a blistering whisper that she could see my *nipples* through my T-shirt. She had given me one of her old bras, teal satin, but you could see down into it that I didn't have enough chest to fill it up.

A shadow passed over my eyes and turned the gloom inside my head from red to green. A boy was standing over me. He was tall and his elbows buckled out to the sides since he had his hands on his hips in a disapproving way.

"Hey. Hey. You better get away from here." I sat up and squinted at him. There were two more boys behind him, and a girl with her hands hitched down into her shorts pockets. Back up at the house, I had missed the white Range Rover. A dark cord flashed across my eyes. Something in my head was ringing, and they came closer. My underwear was drying out and it stuck to my skin when I shifted around.

"Can't you see the sign? Can't you read?" It was posted NO TRESPASSING all around the fence, but I shrugged.

"Course she can't read," the girl said. Her T-shirt sleeves were cuffed up almost perfectly to look like wings.

"I can read," I said. I hated how my voice sounded feathery.

"Then what's she doing here?" the other boy asked. I wished him to say it louder so Virgil would hear and come tell them off. I cut my eyes to the left, where the fishing was, and saw Virgil and Clinton naked except for wet underwear, leaning their heads together over something. The boys were standing on either side of me now, although I did not believe they had the guts to put a hand on me. The boys had white T-shirts that were so bright in the sun they looked blue. The taller one, he was closer and his jaw hung down. He was looking down my bra.

I wanted to scare him. So I took his hand and put it to the front of my underwear. He had to stoop down. But he did it willingly. His palms were cold, and I realized he was already afraid, of me or in that moment, some way. The waistband of my underwear was still wet, but the rest of me was all cooked from the sun. He hardly moved, but a clear drop of snot fell from his nose onto my knee. I pushed his hand down farther to my privates. It was so quiet I thought I heard his fingernail catch on the cotton. I don't know how long we stayed like that.

"Ew, freak!" the girl said. Except she said it long, like: fur-reek. That's how I could tell she wasn't from here. "Whatever, come on." The tall one was still looking at me. He wiped his hand on his shorts like I had messed it. She kicked the shorter boy in the ankle, and that broke the spell. When I stood up they took off hard, running backward for a second before they turned. They crashed the laurels at the lake rim and threw all the birds in there upward. Clinton looked up at the sound. I don't know what he saw. Nothing that worried him, plainly. I got the shampoo from where we had dropped our things and poured a flood of it in my hand, hot like my own guts, and walked back into the water to wash.

It was the kind of gas station where they kept a black rubber hose out front for you to drive over and clang a bell. Virgil and Clinton were about to mow a big field for some gas company that needed a clear plot for a foreman's trailer, and they were excited about the money. We were still drying off from the pond. My hair floated up white blond. The radio was coming in clear that day, Bad Company and Van Halen, although the clouds were metal blue at their edges and it would rain. I felt good. I usually had a window of optimism after I bathed, which wore off by the time I was dry again. But for just then, I was washed. I was hungry in a clean right way I hadn't found in some time.

Inside the gas station was a store that had basically one of everything. All the food was pushed to the edge of the shelf with nothing else behind it, so it looked more like someone's private soup museum than a grocery. People said it was a front for a secret poker game, or possibly the McConaugheys moved pain clinic pills or whatnot. In any case, it had the soft, sour smell of a room no one uses. Each can had a price sticker on the top and was dim from dust, although you could see brighter swipes from where people had picked the thing up, the cocktail weenies or whatever, and considered buying it, and then put it back. I went around writing things in the dust. I wrote *BABIES* on everything. *BABIES BABIES BABIES.*

The girl behind the counter had a deep face, like her eyes were all the way back in there, and she had a line down her chin where she had been glued back together, and her name was Melda McConaughey, which I knew because she and Virgil had been the same year in school. They had actually gone to prom together, although just, Virgil said, as friends. Even though they had only graduated three years before, Melda already looked a little like a mom or an aunt I wouldn't notice. She wore a big sweatshirt with her fingers dangling out of the cuffs, and she had a pink tissue balled up in one fist. When she saw Virgil, she stopped rolling quarters and busted down crying.

"Oh my god," she said. "You heard." *What was this?* I wondered. I loved it when anybody was in grief. Grief was something interesting. It had a heat, and I had none of my own. It seemed to me I hadn't felt anything with a point to it, and yet I cried often. One time I cried at the store over a stuffed chimpanzee shoved in with the magazines. It had probably fallen out of someone's cart. I thought about all the empty hours it would spend, and its lostness. I wasn't stone. Sometimes my sorrow lay over all I saw, like neon light.

"What's the matter?" Virgil asked her. "Is it your mom? Is she OK?"

She waved away the thought. Her mouth was open and she sucked in air while her shoulders racked.

"It's Jude," she said. "She's been missing for weeks, but nobody knew."

"How do you mean?"

"I don't know, I just heard."

"Why you crying about it if you don't know how true it is?" Clinton asked.

"Well, last week they found that other girl in the woods behind the CoGo's. It's terrible!"

Clinton shrugged like maybe it was, maybe it wasn't. "She could've just run away."

"She's dead," Melda said. "I can just feel it. Sometimes I just know things. I knew it as soon as I saw you."

"Whoa," Virgil said.

"You were the one she really loved. You know that? Because it's true. I'm sure she died loving you."

Melda spoke in a fashion borrowed from soap operas, and I thrilled in it. I felt almost a secondary kind of fame from it. I maybe was not that much of anything, but my brother, he was a dead girl's true love. Virgil and Jude had dated for almost two years, which was long for high school. I had always been a little obsessed about her. Sometimes, when I was bored, I would go through my catalogs and pick out a gift for Jude on every page, what I imagined she'd like, anyway, and I had from that the illusion that I knew her well. It says a lot about my interest in Jude that I took her disappearance as some juicy twist instead of danger coming to a real person. I guess I thought of her as a character above anything else. She seemed fearless, even as different from everybody else as she was. I, on the other hand, said strange wrong things almost constantly and burned with the shame of it. So I made her a hero, and sowed meaning in everything she did, but I couldn't accomplish this without making her flat, without real features or pain.

Virgil went behind the counter and he held Melda. Like a little girl she tucked her head into his shoulder. She was still holding the paper sleeves for the quarters, and they rustled as she clasped her hands around his neck. And that was the only sound happening in there. Clouds moved over the sun. The light in the room shrank away.

"You know if anybody's checked on Bernadette?" Virgil said.

"Who's that?" Melda asked.

"That's her mom. Shit. She'll be in pieces."

"Well, I don't know. You go up and ask at Pecjak's. Everybody's talking about it. I heard they set up a TV on the hoagie counter." Just like that, Virgil was already out the door without good-bye. Right away the truck started up. Christ, Clinton said to the hurry.

Sissy Pecjak's gas station had a row of tables inside, so it was something, very slightly, of a restaurant, and you could also buy motor oil, tires, kiddie pools, feather dusters made of real dyed chicken feathers, and everything like that. There was a coffee smell as soon as we got in the door, and it was too hot because so many people were standing around sweating and the smell of wet tobacco and salt and oil and hay came up to punch on my brain. I had never seen so many people there before. It was all men, except for Sissy herself, and she was reaching up to find a pack of cigarettes in the dispenser while her own lit one shook down a cap of ash onto her blouse. The sound of everybody talking went like: *wash, wash, wash.* All the newspaper racks were empty. Virgil asked if anybody'd spare a paper and some bald-headed man with little round glasses and white muttonchops told him he could go find one on the floor of the john. I stood in the back. The refrigerator case leaked hot air on the backs of my legs. Clinton dropped his hands down on my shoulders like they were keeping me from floating away. It was plain that everybody was very excited. On the TV, they showed a picture of Jude from senior skip day. She was sitting on a garbage can in front of the Sheetz with a backward baseball cap and an extra-large Mountain Dew and very stylish round sunglasses. If you didn't know her, you might think she was tough, but she played violin and read poems on the morning announcements. Still, all the men standing around were muttering about she must have gotten herself into some bad business, dealing drugs like her kind usually did. But what they really meant was: She was black. Well, mixed, but in Greene County that meant basically the same thing, and she was the only black person in school. Her father, Alistair Vanderjohn, was a college professor and a black man, all at once. Whenever he came to visit, you could feel the effort people made to not stare, just like you could feel us all move our eyes around Jude.

The people standing around were saying the Vanderjohn girl had been gone two weeks at the slightest, and she'd run away because her momma was a hoarder and a bestiality practicer, and someone had seen Jude in the Greene Plaza shopping center, which was where people waited in their cars to buy dope from other people in cars. And someone else said oh my god she was just there to buy those chocolate bars from the Aldi's that everybody's so crazy about. Well, I'm just saying. Well. It sure is sad, is what they were all saying. It's so sad. What a tragedy, so young, and all this, except their eyes were glass burned up with joy, with the kind of light you don't see except in happy people. I swear it. Someone had even brought a cooler of beers inside the store like this was all for fun. I couldn't understand why people's faces were matched so badly to their words. Except of course I could. Everybody loved a tragedy, especially me.

The bald-headed man leaned up next to Clinton and said, "Can't believe it, but it happens all the time."

"Yup."

"You better watch out for that one. She's old enough to worry about, sure." His eyes landed on me, wet and shivery, I guess because of some emotion. I didn't like how they stuck on my chest.

"Oh no, Cindy's good, she stays at home and helps. Huh, bunny?" I could feel right then how my belly poured out over my shorts and my T-shirt kept rolling up over it, and how my legs were crammed together with sweat at the top. I would give anything to disappear.

"Well, that's good. That's *remarkable*." The last part he said louder, so I knew he was trying to talk to me. When he turned away, I wrote *F-U-C-K-Y-O-U* on my arm with a fingernail.

Virgil was back with the newspaper. It had been folded so the pages were all shuffled up and had wavered from water drying. His mouth was plucked down at the edges, and he looked a little wild in the eye. He bought a candy bar anyway since it would be rude to not buy anything. A Caramello, which he handed off to me like no big deal, but he knew they were my favorites. I carried it lightly by its edges so the heat from my hands wouldn't ruin it. I would eat it alone in my room, and if I did it right I would briefly begin to float.

I don't know, and maybe I just wanted the attention, but disappearing didn't seem so awful to me. I liked the thought of it, right away. I know that sounds cold, but I wanted so badly to be gone. She had passed to another side where there was no accounting for her actions, and where there was nobody to talk at her. I wished I had thought to go missing.

And I wanted to be famous. I wanted all the hidden hearts to search for me. I wanted to sparkle in the vast outline of the gone, because the gone took up the whole sky and air. How had Jude done this magic? Gone was a place where nobody could touch you. Like a heaven, or that's what I thought.

Pulling away from Pecjak's, a new cold edge came on the air. The road spooled out backward from my spot in the truck bed. Each curve ate the last gray curve, and when we dipped the silvery trees and signs and things were whipped clean away by our motion. I imagined Jude carried off by a vast wind, scattering the treetops as she passed. The storm broke, and threw cold coins of water down on me in the back of the pickup.

III

The first time I really noticed Jude, I was little, maybe ten or eleven. It was a summer day, blind and hot. Through the vines, I could see the dogs moving in the bowers. Grapes hung down between their legs, little ones, and their backs were black. The air and sun lit up their edges blond. They went in circles or turned back to pace. A green car went through, a black truck, a blue truck. I was watching them all morning.

My brothers mowed yards for money every spring and summer, but I had always been confined, unfairly, to the house and the porch. I counted the cars, all the kinds and colors, for something to do, but it was a hobby with a lot of boredom in it.

"Get me out a piece of bread, Cindy," Virgil said that particular day. He was a senior in high school then. He had come in from mowing and the seeds dandled off his arm hairs and stuck to his sweat. His shirt was all stretched out. He wiped the grease on his chest like a V.

"She ain't supposed to be fetching for you," Mom said. She was in the kitchen smacking can icing down onto a sheet cake with a butter knife. Clinton was in the dark on the couch just waking up. He threw his arms wide and wiggled the fingers.

"Fuck if you would," Clinton said. "Give me something."

She brought a pie out from the icebox and my brothers took into it with their forks and ate the whole thing down to the tin in two silent minutes.

"She said anything today?" Virgil asked and lit his cigarette.

"She's been watching cars," Mom said. "I don't know."

"Was you watching cars, sweetness?" I had my head leaned on the wood lip of the door frame, and softly, softly, I smacked my temple on it, just from being bored crazy. Sometimes I pressed in soft places on my head just to see the color flashes. Virgil put his smoke down in the pie pan and tilted it around in a circle so the tip was a dark gray cone. He focused on that, and blew out hard. "I got another house lined up. The Satterwhite lady. The one with all the wind chimes down the hill? She wants the grass done this afternoon."

"She wants the grass done every afternoon," Mom said. "I thought you was down there yesterday."

"If she wants to pay, I don't mind it. Her business." He stretched and ran his hands over his ribs.

"You just go over there at night, paint it all green. Bet you she'd never notice."

"Afternoon," Clinton said, and sucked his teeth. "Is what it already is."

"We got to go now, is what I'm saying."

"Man, I can't. I'm too bored to think about it." Clinton prayed his hands together and pulled his hair down over his face in a stiff blond spike.

"You better take her with," Mom said, and flapped her hand toward me. "I got to not be stared at for a minute today."

The window light blazed around them and they were dark with just some edges. Clinton peeled off his glasses and butted his wrists into his eyes to grind out the sleep sand, the little moon-green boogers. We all got them, as a family. A rind of heat was singing through the screen door and I wandered to it. A black truck went down the road. It was so black it was green, but it wasn't our truck. The woman driving it had a red ponytail and little round sunglasses. She looked long at the house when she went by but she couldn't see us. I didn't think so. I made a grocery sack with my things in it. I didn't get to leave the house all that much. For all I knew we were going away a long time.

Virgil pushed the mowers up on boards that ramped into the truck bed, shoved the boards up after. He boosted me onto the tailgate with his two big hands on my ribs. They held the heat of the sun, or maybe it was his blood that did it. I shimmied crabwise back into the hay dust that gathered in the black grooves and put my back against the window into the cab. Mom was laying more boxes on the burn pile. Her head had disappeared behind the scary milk that came off the fire.

The truck shook when Virgil turned it on. My tailbone buzzed from it. Clinton came falling out of the house. The way he walked, his legs just caught up in time to keep him from tipping. He had a baseball cap on backward and the plaid shirt flew open so I could see his shoulders where the undershirt cut away. He was always sleeping in his glasses. They left a deep red line across the bridge of his nose. He had put a bottle of pink wine down in his back pocket. He touched it to make sure it was still there.

"Shit. Shit!" Virgil clapped twice. He turned up the radio. He looked back out at me and winked.

The road had grass grown up in its middle between the tire tracks. It bowed under us as we went out along the ridge. We turned onto a paved road that took us down from the hill spine. At the bottom there was a proper painted road with the yellow lines and some mailboxes off it. I couldn't hear the music in the cab very clear. Virgil and Clinton smoked from the pack of USA Gold on the dash. My hair made a stinging cloud. It whipped around my face. I tried to gather it in a hand and hold it but gave up and let it whip into my eyes and stick on my lips.

The house sat back on a stamped-down run of grass that looked to not need cutting. It was a bruised green from being mown already. A husky dog folded its paws one over the other on the porch. It stood when our truck crawled up onto the gravel, but the woman on the porch put her hand flat on its back and it sat again. Across the road some goats were picking across a whole field of mud, all the flat part along the crick churned up from their hooves. They held very still, but with their tails fluttering.

I jumped down and set the ramp boards like I had seen Virgil do it always, but he moved them a little, moved them back. He waved at the woman, and she came toward us with her hand visoring her eyes. Her dress was long and the grass pulled it back as she walked so it spread behind her like a train on a bride, which I thought was very pretty. She moved like there was juice in her bones and nothing to hurry about. I know it now: It's the way people walk when they like what they are. But I had never seen it before. She wore a bunch of purple tin bracelets with diamond shapes bit out of them. Her tan went right up under her clothes and didn't have the ghost edges of a T-shirt anywhere. My mother was also tan, but in the reverse of the low-cut shirt she wore every day. Mom's chest was a brown, wrinkled plat the shape of the mat they put down in the batter's box.

"Back already?" she asked Virgil.

"We ran out of gas the other day. Didn't get the edges of that back field."

"Well, how kind of you to return. I probably wouldn't even notice. I'm about to fix us BLTs, if you'd like a plate when you're done?" I started to walk up to the woman with the skittering bracelets because I wanted BLTs right away, but Clinton stayed me with a hand on my chest.

"Oh, your little girl can come in the house," she said. "It's too hot to leave her outside."

"She's our sister."

"She waits in the truck," Clinton said, squinting at her.

"Well, on the porch, at least." She was used to getting her way. I could tell. She ducked her head so she could look at my eyes. "Honey, you like doggies?" I nodded.

I jumped down and she pushed me along with her hand flat on my shoulders. It was like she could steer me by invisible strings. I wanted to do just whatever she wanted me to.

The dog was named Mondo and it had a teddy bear face, all one color. She showed me how to let Mondo smell my hand before I patted him on the head. He let me push his ears around in circles, but when she went inside, he walked away with his tail hanging right down, like he was done for the day with pretending to be a dog.

Inside there was a girl with her hair pulled back tight across her head. She was edging inside the window with a paintbrush. The way the light hit her glasses made her eyes just blanks. This was Jude, of course. I knew her a little from the school bus. She was always putting on her deodorant as the bus churned away from her house, and when she slipped it up inside her sweater I could see a slice of her stomach.

Jude must have been fourteen, a freshman at West Greene. She was the kind of person who seemed older than the teachers sometimes. Once, there had been a competition at school to know math in your head, which they made us all watch. She had won, I remember, but she looked bored the whole time. When she was thinking up the answers, she balanced on one leg with her head tilted down, as if she barely needed to think. She wasn't like anyone else. Everything she did, surely it was the coolest thing to do because she did it. If I tried, I came off like a freak. I did not know the origin of this curse, but I was so thirsty to know that I cursed myself, I'm sure, even more.

She was looking right at me, on the porch, so I waved at her. She brought a cigarette up to her lips and blew the smoke out through her nostrils. Had she seen me? It seemed like she had not. I was surprised she was smoking in the house. At school she was a brain, and brains supposedly did not do stuff like that. But then she heard the side door open and she dropped the cigarette in a water glass and pushed it out of sight. "Mondo, hey, no," she said. Her voice fell as she walked away.

I took out my games and the mowers crossed over each other droning like two people having a conversation about unrelated things. And then something happened in my head where I couldn't like my toys anymore. I was getting too old for games, but nobody knew what to do with me. Neither did I. My mom used to pet the bridge of my nose and whisper me gossip stories when I couldn't sleep, but one day she just stopped, and would stay in her bedroom with the air conditioner running, and have headaches. I had a wood paddle with a rubber ball on a string stapled to it and a tube made out of the plastic plaid from lawn chairs that you could trap your whole thumbs inside. My doll would not hold up her head. Her head was on a stick that went down into her soft body and I had broken the stick when I rolled over on it sleeping too hard. I wanted for her to be restored. She would just rest her head on her chin for all the rest of time. I felt disappointed by her. I felt like she had been dipped in oil. My hands made prints on her neck. I was too old for dolls, but I still saw them as alive. What would they do when I abandoned them? They could not go to work or have children to distract themselves. It made me so sad I got my breath stuck in my throat and thought I could cry.

The lady came outside with a glass of orange juice and it had ice cubes in it. She put it down next to me and sat on the edge of the porch. There was no sandwich, but neither did I want to ask about it. Mondo trotted up, on duty again. She ran a wire brush over his back and blew the fur balls so they caught in the air and sailed away.

"Your brothers work really hard."

Clinton would be stealing a sip from the wine bottle under the truck seat if she would just go inside. He slapped the sweat off his face and turned his glare away since I was watching him.

"What's your name?" she asked.

"Cindy," I said. I looked very hard at my doll. She had pink circles on her face, and brown braids.

"Do you want to brush him?" she asked. "He likes it."

I knee-walked over to her and she steered the brush in my hand. It left furrows in the dog's back. When I ran the brush over the bones of his haunches his head jerked and swiveled like a broken toy.

"It's OK. It doesn't hurt him. His nerves are coming back to life. The people who had him before kept him in a box and he didn't get to use his legs."

We kept brushing him until a smell compelled Mondo elsewhere. She got up, too, and walked off, twisting up her hair. The hills went out in waves. The faraway ones were blue from all the water held up in the air. I jumped down from the side of the porch to follow the lady and the dog, but instead I saw Virgil leaning with an arm up above his head, buckling his fingers on the tree bark so the tips were yellow-white. He kept his hair long on top. The back of his neck was buttered from sweat. He tilted his head in like he was listening to a tiny trumpet off in the distance. No, he was kissing her. Jude had her hands folded behind her back, against the tree trunk. It looked artificial, like she would in a second recite a poem from memory. It was the first time I had seen two people try to eat each other up like that. And it worked. They were both gone. They were replaced with this wavering image.

Jude opened her eyes and caught me watching. Her stare pinned me to the earth. The mower was still running. It jigged ahead like a sleepwalker. Virgil must have felt her attention switch because the next thing he stepped back to the Lawn-King and resumed like nothing had happened just then. But I couldn't move.

It was probably not such a long time that Jude and I stood there, staring at each other, but I got lost in it. Sky-blue paint speckled her face like stardust. I would have taken all the fingernails out of my hands to look so elegant and possible as she did. Then my head went thick from a sudden stillness, and I realized the lawnmower engines had been cut. Out by the truck I heard Virgil setting the boards and Clinton pulling both mowers behind him. The grass was like a washed thing. If you could drink it, it would fix you and all your bruises would fall off, and all your freckles and bug bites. Clinton pissed on a tree. The crape myrtle hid his hips.

"Cindy. Come on," Virgil yelled at me from the driveway. Jude was trying to cross her arms but could not seem to keep still. "Um," I said, and then she walked away. So I ran up on the porch. The ice cubes in my orange juice were gone to almost nothing and I sucked them up into my teeth. It was one of my best games. I would freeze my jaw stiff chewing on ice and then feel the muscles seize up. I was hoping the woman would come back out and put her hand on my shoulders again before we left.

"Cindy. Leave it," he shouted, and threw the truck into gear. I put the dog brush in with my things. I don't know why, but I wanted it. There was a blur of mouse-color hair stuck in the wire. When I got home, I would trail it along my arm, to feel the shivers.

I went across the wet shady spots. Heat was in the grass and it bled a little fume of green onto my sneakers. I had to jump up onto the tailgate by myself. It took a few tries, and as soon as I was in we were backing down the driveway, swinging wide.

Clinton brought the bottle out from its dark, but right away had to stow it again. The lady hung there in his window and he cursed a long, grumbling word. She had come running out when she heard the truck going. Behind her, I saw Jude was back on the porch and she had a violin grabbed up under her chin. The bow chopped down, two strings by two. She was tuning it. I could tell she was waiting for us to leave.

"That was fast," the woman said. "You want forty? You said forty?"

"Yes, ma'am," Virgil said, ducking to look at her. He must have been really scared about getting caught kissing, because Virgil never forgot to get paid.

She pulled two folded bills from what seemed like behind her back, like a card trick. I wondered if she had hidden them next to her skin. Or did she always and that's where her money came from. There were little globes of white in her armpits and her hair was red on top where the sun was getting at it.

Clinton put the money in the glove box and waved a two-finger goodbye at her, and Virgil let the truck jump away down the road. It spit gravel. Some hit the lofting folds of her dress and sent out billows. Like the curtains in a theater, I thought, when somebody in a cartoon would throw a rotted cabbage at the singer who trilled the high notes too hard. It looked like she didn't have any legs under there. The lady frowned. She was going to say something to me. I have always wondered what. But the time when I would know Bernadette was years off at that point. Whatever she was going to say, I saw her swallow it back down as the gravel popped under our tires. And she got smaller and smaller. Or we got smaller and smaller. Mondo ran out in the road and barked at us leaving. He followed some ways and then, satisfied by our defeat, turned and hobbled back home. I lay on my back and let the sky tear itself up between the leaves, and then the trees closed in and I was returned to the green dark place where I belonged.

My mother was not very old when she had us. She had been on a school trip to Disney World when she got pregnant with Virgil. She was in the marching band, and everybody in the marching band had to go on the trip, even though it was expensive. They tried to make it fair by having everybody sell candy bars from flimsy cardboard suitcases with plastic handles that always fell off by the end of the first day.

But it wasn't fair at all. Nobody in her school—which was also my school—had a lot of money, but some kids got their parents to buy up all the right number of candy bars and the family would put them in the freezer to eat on for the rest of the year, until the next band trip. My mother sold all her candy bars herself. She got rides into town to sell them in front of the Giant Eagle and walked along the strip of dentist offices and the lab places by the hospital where they draw your blood and spin it apart. Really, it was a pretty good idea to go to the dentist offices, where people were walking out with those new teeth that your tongue just slips over.

She had never been out of state, unless you count West Virginia, which you shouldn't, because it's the same as the place we are from in landscape and custom and all of that, and how people talk, and what they call a good idea.

So it was an exciting thing for her. They went around in a park with smaller versions of Europe, little German picture bracelets and Spanish leather coin purses and white-skirted dancing maidens. There were fireworks every night, lagoon rides. And so many other people, people who you could see once and then never again.

Everybody was to stay in groups of three. My mother's group followed the letter of this rule but not its intention, and they found three boys who were just park rats with nothing better to do than hang out with them. Park boyfriends. They held hands in line for the water rides. The boys stole them cups that had a waterfall of blue goo and glitter trapped inside. At the end of each day, they planned what landmark they would meet at the next morning, and every morning the vow renewed at the World of Motion, the Universe of Energy.

At that point is where my mother would start skipping parts of the story because she didn't want me to know anything about the rest of it, how you find a soft spot where the shadows are thick and the shredded bark mulch is feathery. And how all the other things. How the two people are thinking so hard about getting their clothes off, and how terrible their clothes are, getting caught on everything, elbows, heels, the way a person's jeans button is backward from where you're used to finding it on your own body. And how everything about the experience is backward because there is now somebody else sucked into the bubble where you live, and they are like you but different, and if you just met them yesterday you still can't really remember their face when you close your eyes, except in these small flashes, and those are too lovely to let you breathe at all.

She was still in school. She kept on going right until the last month. When she finally dropped out, it wasn't because she complained. It bothered people too much to look at her. Mrs. Donnerbrau let her stay in the home ec room during lunch to make baby clothes, and some of the girls talked to her at the lockers like nothing was new, but in gym class, they gave her a red dodge ball and put her out to wait in the hallway until the bell to change clothes rang. Like a dog. Everybody wanted to give her privacy while she changed back into her shorts with the big elastic patch and her WVU sweatshirt, which was all she wore every day, except that they would die of not looking. The veins on her belly were big and green. You could see straight through her skin, of course.

And that is the story of Virgil.

Clinton's daddy was another man. He had been in jail for cracking a parking garage attendant over the head with a bag of sugar. My mom was cleaning hotel rooms at the time, and they met because he was refilling the vending machines. They saw each other at the same time every week, and then that day became the best day of the week, they both looked nicest that day although they could hardly talk because they were both already laughing at what the other one was saying. He drove her everywhere. She had never been so in motion in her life. He had a jack parakeet that lived in his truck. It was a whole world in there. They took Virgil to Lake Erie and went out to dinner in places where they brought around a silver barge of desserts at the end, and it turned out that his money was all from life insurance scams and he left in the middle of the night, in the middle of one of their trips, and my mother hitchhiked back from the Smoky Mountains with Virgil crying on her hip. She got carsick all over some nun's LeBaron. When she got home, she kept getting carsick, even when she wasn't going anywhere.

And that is the story of Clinton.

She was drinking then. She got herself a parakeet. Its name was Bandit, and it was no help. Its favorite thing to do was to sit in a paper bag inside its cage. Virgil remembers how she'd slam the furniture if they were crying. She never touched them. But if they were crying while all of whatever was going on, she would pick up the nearest piece of furniture and let it crash back in place. That was about when she stopped drinking, too. She was going to find it in the church, the don't-kill-yourself. That's when she was putting Virgil in the pageants. She was taking GED class and had all kinds of pamphlets for learning how to take blood out of people's bodies, which was a good job, and she was trying and praying, and the most incredible thing happened. The boy from the amusement park came back. Virgil's daddy. Not back, maybe: He was a missionary visiting her church to talk about praying into a positive attitude, teaching a six-week course about the science of the Christian mind. They weren't even sure how they knew each other at first. Of course a lot of things had happened to him. He had been in the navy. He had found the church because of his wife, but she had died in a complicated birth and so he found more church from the grief of it. That my mother was there in front of him, and that she had already survived the delivery of their son, was nothing but miracle. He came over for dinner the next day with a football for Virgil, gave the boys that one required spiral lesson: fingers on the stitches, watch how it spins in the blue. He came over for dinner the next day again. One of those gruff blond men, he must have a heart in there somewhere. He brought her flowers. She made steaks and peach cobbler, paid elaborate attention to her hair.

I guess it was the miracle talk that got to her, because what a miracle meant to my mother was: the end of suffering. Finally the world could be forgiven, now that it made sense. It had shown itself a bully but who didn't know about that? Defeated, it spread its plush belly before her. Here it was: the true pure gold. This man's love would save her forever. She wasn't cleaning hotel rooms anymore. She worked at the coffee shop in the hospital. Everything in the air had a taste. Eternity, French fries, leatherette, bleach. She was drinking again. It was fine now. World of Motion. Universe of Energy.

I don't know what happened. Something changed in the weather between them and he decided to leave when the six weeks were over. I've cut it every way I could think to: She drank too much, Clinton was a brat, he never meant it, he was afraid. Maybe it was too much to go from no family to family fully assembled overnight. Maybe he was just one of those who can't like any one thing for very long. Maybe he and my mother had simply never discussed what they meant to each other. Maybe he never meant to stay. But he went off on another mission trip. She felt she couldn't show her face again, so that was the end of church. She sued for child support.

One day, she was in line behind Bernadette Satterwhite at the Giant Eagle. Bernadette always looked like an actress, or someone who had ideas of herself. She wore a belly shirt and a black skirt with little round mirrors sewn around the hem. She had Jude on her hip and a big leather purse and tortoise sunglasses. She paid for her food and asked the bagger to take her things out to the truck, a thing which nobody else ever did. She gave her girl a quarter for the magic egg machine. And then she turned around to my mother and said, "I'm one of the indigo children. I'm blessed with second sight, and honey, that baby inside you is already dead."

"You're a lying B from H-E-double," my mother said, because she had a thing against cusses. Of course there was no baby. She'd just put on weight from eating through hangovers. She felt like hell, but who didn't? Two months later, I was born into the toilet at the Greene County Memorial Hospital, where my mother was hiding out on her break from making coffee for all those bald doctors. Miracle talk, all over again. But my daddy, Virgil's daddy, didn't ever write back. It had been too much the first time. Nobody needed more proof.

And that is the story of me.

IV

Somebody who knew somebody at the sheriff's office told the Pecjak's crowd that Jude's car had been towed to Gebe & Skocik Tire in Uniontown. The garage was empty that day on account of a Pirates game. The tow company's paperwork had been filled out in a rushed and cruddy way, so it was difficult to say who had picked her up. Detective Torboli asked all the drivers if they remembered getting a girl in Gans the middle Sunday of May. It seemed like it should not be so hard to remember, but they claimed they couldn't even say for sure what they had done just that morning. There were calls all the time, you got the people, the lights changed in the edges of the sky. Such mysteries. Who knows.

When they searched Jude's car, they found a JanSport backpack with a bottle of vodka in it, a baggie of stems in the glove box, stepped-on geometry homework, and a notebook of swears in French, but no money or ID.

It got around that the day bartender at O'Gillie's had seen on that day a girl matching Jude's description who wanted to order a gin and tonic in a tall glass but claimed she'd left her ID somewhere when asked for it. He served her an iced tea but later found her sitting with a middle-aged man at a back table drinking a pitcher and feeding French fries to a poodle tied up under the table. He said he'd thrown them both out then. When police showed him the photograph of Jude for comparison, he said it was possibly the same girl he had seen, but he could have sworn she was Brandy someone or other whose father owned the local septic empire and tried to drink on the infamy even though she wasn't legal. But perhaps he was mistaken. They all look the same to me, he said, although it wasn't clear if he meant black girls or underage ones. He seemed to recall she had a lot of cash on her. He felt certain she had worn a feather in her hair, one of those dyed chicken feather roach clips you win at the fair.

At the house across the street from Gebe & Skocik, the fentanyl addicts were sitting out in yellow sweatshirts bought bulk that advertised the Mountaineers winning the Sugar Bowl in '94, which they had not. All of them were saying they had seen Jude. They had seen a girl. A girl, once, and she wasn't very nice. Was this Jude? She had headed over to bum a smoke. She had a bruise on her clavicle and kept her sunglasses on. She had a feather in her hair. She had no feather. Her hair was wet. Wet hair looked like a damn piece of ink or seaweed. Her dog didn't seem to like her. Her dog was a little chow. There was no dog. She was wearing a parka with the tags still on it. She had walked off in the direction of the Dunkin' Donuts. She had stayed with them, like family. She had died in their arms.

One of them claimed he knew her from violin camp when they were kids. His name was Dustin Gehoe. He had won first chair in the West Liberty University Children's Orchestra. Jude was second chair. He had eyes with all the shine shook out of them, but nice manners. They had been pen pals. He had once sent Jude a matryoshka doll. What did it mean? Detective Torboli had taken a statement, hopeless though it must have seemed.

But really, I hadn't been the only one who paid such close attention to Jude. We would all become collectors of Jude minutiae, and trade scraps of the known and the overheard and the fathomed without really caring what any of it meant. Maybe everyone in Greene County believed they would solve the case this way, but wasn't it more like watching a soap opera? Except better, of course, because if you had known Jude or shared some minor moment with her, you could step into the story yourself, as the wise and now sadder human who must go on living. Everyone from Dustin Gehoe to the lady who drove our school bus made it sound like Jude had tendered a hidden truth of her soul to their confidence, and they held it up to flatter themselves in its sorrowful light. I take a dim view of the practice myself. But I'm also a hypocrite, and fully a part of life on the earth.

The suspects they brought in for questioning were, down to the dime and penny, compromised and illegally inclined and born out of waves of these wrong ways, iron cross tattoos, bad ideas about women, burned knuckles. They were almost boasting about it at Sissy Pecjak's gas station. People gave Tanner Fordyce all kinds of shit around the sandwich counter because he seemed like the only grown man who hadn't been interviewed for the investigation, and was he turning puss on them, or what? Maybe the trouble was that the police did not know anything save for the day when the abduction had occurred, so there was no narrowing of fact. No telling details coincided. Not to mention all the men they brought in were happily confessing to little-bit schemes they could swear to have been in the commission of at the appointed hour, no matter what hour that might be. One willingly acknowledged he had been holed up in an Econo Lodge in little Washington that whole weekend shooting dope into his girlfriend's neck, and then set a slot machine on fire when he nodded out with his cigarette hand on the MORE button at the Meadows. Plenty reels of closed-circuit footage bore out the truth of this statement.

The girls had made it home in time for the wedding. They told the whole thing over and over through the night: the blackberry wine. B.D.'s eyes flushed pink like a rabbit's. They had about them the glamour of the nearly killed, and they would not set it aside for anything. It was not just any day that they had been in such danger. Morgan, the bride, was furious. Everybody in the ersatz beauty parlor of her prefab was talking about whether Jude would make it back in time for the wedding, and here was Morgan in her dress already, with nobody talking about that.

During the ceremony, when she appeared at the back of the church, the assembled turned to watch her, it was true, but many of them turned also to see if Jude was there in the back of the room as she had not yet seated herself.

It was not the best wedding. A few things went wrong. The bride and groom could not get the unity candle to light, even though Morgan had expressly asked that the church's HVAC be turned off for the duration of the ceremony to address this need. The former footballers got sweat-pinched in the stiff collars of their church clothes. The groom's mother swilled on blank Chardonnay in the cocktail hour and began to talk loudly about the tribulations of her own marriage, which had been alive only in bickering and back rubs for the last twenty years. At the head table, an extra place setting had been stuffed in to accommodate a second cousin who had not RSVP'd or participated in any of the wedding party activities but showed up, nevertheless, in her own home-sewn version of the bridesmaid gown.

The guests spoke of nothing but the girls' near brush with disaster. Some speculated that they knew just which boys had chased them. It was the Whipkey brothers, certainly, or the Polands or the Masons. Everybody, it seemed, knew a clan of bad seeds who hung out in those woods. Were they wearing matching flannels? Did they have stick-poke tattoos of the Eye of Horus? Were they drinking Night Train? Things like this.

Some thought it might even be Virgil and Clinton Stoat, never mind their more or less permanent sequester up on Wildman Run Road. Never mind that they numbered but two—they lived in one of those ivy-strangled houses cocooned with POW/MIA flags and the spikes of scanner radios along the roof. That's how people talked about us. I know, because sometimes people forgot I was a Stoat, too. And sometimes they just forgot we might be able to hear them. That night, I was making rounds with a lemonade pitcher and taking plates at the reception—it was a one-time job Virgil had got us because he knew the cater lady, though he got to stay in the kitchen making urns of coffee while I showed around my invisible smile and scraped chicken bones into the big drum of a garbage can, which could have fit my whole body.

And nobody said so, of course, but the clatter of rented silverware and chimed water glasses hushed every time somebody opened the door to the fellowship hall. Everyone looked to see if it was Jude, showing herself late and maybe dewy, straight from the shower, with her long black dress and her usual tin bracelets zithering around on her wrists. But no.

The mother of the groom threw up on her plate when the cake was passed. Some uncle was found hiding out in a stall of the ladies' restroom, claiming he was there to fix a broken toilet bobber. And it had rained, a cold and heavy slapping kind of rain all through the jeweled trees around the church, littering branches over the cars, and the guests arrived at the reception with their hair all upset looking and mascara soot run down their cheeks. Good luck, everybody said. That it must be good luck for rain on such a wedding.

And still, it had taken another week before Jude was even reported missing. The girls, it seemed, presumed she had come home too late to make the reception, too tired or over it to dress herself up in time. Crystal called the house a few times to check on her friend. She left messages with Bernadette, who said Jude would be gone a few days and would call back soon.

One afternoon, Kayla had apparently stopped by Jude's house. She was taking her little cousins up to Burns Delite for ice cream and wanted the company, or, more honestly, wanted the help. Trey and Ray and Rita were ice-blond and violent children. Everything was guns and bombs and peeing and toilets and they left nasty red scratches all over each other. Bernadette came to the dark screen door but wouldn't step out onto the porch with all the hitting and thrashing. Why, Jude was off camping with her friends, she said. Yes, in Coopers Rock. They wouldn't be home until Sunday, for the wedding.

Kayla tried to explain, but the conversation halted every time she told Bernadette that she herself had gone on the camping trip and come back a week ago and the wedding was over, that Jude had a car problem and had been stranded in Gans.

"Gans?" Bernadette said. "No, that's not right. They were going to Coopers Rock."

Kayla hauled her little cousins back home again and called the police. But it was Sunday. The officer she spoke with suggested that the missing girl was more likely off with a new boyfriend or otherwise engaged recreationally. Perhaps she was ruled by a dark planet? Likely she was doing some drugs. He must have sounded like a man who had driven a long way in the dark to end up where he was. Nobody would want to go halfway across the county to scare up a girl likelier engaged in vodka spacetime travel. And why wasn't the mother making the call? Although in some matters, I'm told, the police take measure by what alarms the friends rather than the parents; otherwise they'd just shake up the same thin-skulled junkie kids over and over for chugging cough syrup behind the Giant Eagle, getting lost in the colors of the music that shook from their poorly maintained Pontiacs. Greene County has a heroin problem. It's as likely to suck up the kids you'd never suspect as the ones who have been imperiled lifelong. Just the week before, the football coach's grandson had tried to rob Rush's Grocery & Video in Rogersville. He said he had a gun, but it was just his fingers shaped like one. Ruthie Rush whacked his hand with her bar-code scanner, and he ran out of there so fast he lost his shoes.

The detective gave Kayla the phone number for his direct line and advised that she call again the next day if a night and a sleep had not settled her mind.

But still, none of the girls heard from Jude. They must have wondered, but she was like that sometimes. She had a stormy inner life, according to Kayla. Sometimes she would seem angry at them for reasons they didn't understand, or fall in love with a boy she'd throw over in three weeks. Her obsessions were flashing but deep: Jack Nicholson in his prime, Romanesque religious art, the movie *Network*, nineties Nancy Drew books. And Nina Simone. Nina Simone. Nina Simone. Later on, I would know these well. It was hard not to. Even though there was so much to do in the house, I would spend much of my days reading through Jude's things. Her bedroom was messed with piled-up treasure, vaguely chronological. The top layer was sort of aspirational. I could tell she had been trying to read *Tess of the d'Urbervilles* for a long time because the first twenty pages had been dog-eared and unfolded, and because it had been arranged on her nightstand with a hurricane candle and a blackened rose. But I could also tell she really loved *Valley of the Dolls*, hidden under her pillow. The spine was loose, the edges foxed up like velvet, and there were all kinds of bookmarks—a carbon copy of an intake form from the free clinic, a goose feather, a piece of gum foil helixed and flattened. And so her friends didn't worry at first. It was summer, and in summer Jude almost always tried to become another person, at least for a little while. By August she usually got tired of trying and she'd watch TV again, gossip again, paint her toenails, enjoy whatever skimming silly pleasure she had sworn off. Amber, who was the most jealous, took things strictly sideways and said Jude had probably hooked up with the tow truck driver. Or the old boy from Burchinal's General Store.

I liked Kayla. She was the only one who didn't make up a story about why Jude was out of contact, and eventually she called the detective again to insist they open a file. Even months after the police had unofficially closed the case, she wouldn't let it go. Sometimes I would run into her at Pecjak's, and we'd stay talking by the hoagie counter, scuffing our shoes on the linoleum to keep ourselves going.

"I just feel like if I go back, I could find her and she wouldn't be gone," she would say. "We should've never left her there. It was a terrible thing to do."

And I would tell her that sometimes, when I felt bad, I would just imagine the worst thing happening over and over until it got muscles, until it ran off the tracks, until it became completely monstrous and unbelievable, and then it wouldn't be so bad. I had a waking dream that went on and on. It was a figure with big dark shoulders and it came into my bedroom. Nothing was worse than the moment before it kissed me.

It swung its chin down and moved like liquid while my life exploded in lights, lights, trying to figure a way out. Trying like this was worse, which it knew, and so it looped itself. Again the big dark shoulders coming in, the liquid and swoop as it moved down to kiss me. It would not leave until I had given up and let it fall upon me and possess me completely.

Bread was the main thing we could not manage to keep enough of in the house, even when Virgil got three entire loaves, one to eat right away and two to go in the freezer chest. We were crazy for bread. We made mayonnaise sandwiches. I sometimes put lettuce on mine when we had it, but they were mostly mayonnaise. Or I rolled them up single pieces in my hands until they were just white balls, heavy to chew through. They left white bits of stickum in my teeth because my teeth went all ways in my mouth.

The problem with the frozen bread was we got a taste for that, too. All three of us, although I thought I was the only one doing it at first. Virgil and Clinton were always hungry from work. I was hungry just from being tired of myself, and the sun. The inside of our house would be invisible in the dark, after being outside, and then it would turn green and then I would see my brothers digging through the pantry for whatever was left. Donald Duck orange juice, all the time. We had a raft of cans that never ran out. I got cankers in the low parts of my gums, and I had a bad tooth in the back of my mouth that whined and sang and made me like it more, somehow, to eat frozen things. But after Jude disappeared, Virgil was spending all day at Bernadette's house, trying to help her get through her grief, and he stopped paying the electricity. Then we just ate from cans or what didn't need any preparation. It was like camping, except inside a house.

Did everybody else know where she was? I didn't like my mother, and I worried anyway. Sometimes I imagined her alone in a hotel room, trying to find her glasses. Or I imagined her on a dark street, on her hands and knees, trying to find her glasses. It was the only way I could feel a pang. And when I couldn't feel a pang, I felt nothing at all.

I didn't like eating. It was the only thing that I liked, so I was depressed when it was over, even though it was the only thing. My tongue felt like a parasite apart from me, a lonely creature wandered far from its ancient ocean. I didn't eat for as long as I could stand. I drank pop instead. I drank so much pop I couldn't taste water anymore. It was too brackish. I realize that sounds unusual or unhealthy, but also the water where we lived smelled like eggs. It left hard white rings around the glass. You'd need a scrub brush to get them off, but why do that when the rings would come back again the next day? So I didn't. Even though I was responsible for washing the dishes, I sometimes just rinsed them and let them dry and nobody had a problem with it.

One day I walked all the way to Pecjak's by myself. The air from the cars going by lifted my hair. Sometimes Sissy pretended she needed a corner swept and let me do it, and paid me in Cheetos or whatever. It was less cute now than it had been when I was ten, and I could tell she kind of didn't want to let me anymore. We couldn't pretend I was of any actual help. But I kept going because while she made my take-home bag of food, I could usually steal something more exciting. It made us even, I had decided. She got to pity me, and I got my ice cream bars. That day I was so hungry that anything I ate passed right through and didn't stick. I was so hungry I had a stitch up my side and I had to walk a little leaned over. I wasn't picking up my feet right. I kept skidding my toe on the road from walking heavy.

There was a man I had never seen before in the restaurant part of the store. Sissy stood over him at a booth with a memo pad in her hand like a waitress, which she never did. Usually, you ordered at the counter, you paid, and then you sat—*in that order*, she would not hesitate to tell you. I recognized him from the TV—he was Jude's dad, although I might have known anyway because I had never seen a black man in Sissy Pecjak's store. It was strange, seeing someone I had never seen before. I know that sounds dumb, but in places like where I'm from, you really do know everybody, so it was a little thrilling. I knew he was some kind of pastor, but he wasn't wearing anything religion-y, just a short-sleeved shirt buttoned up to the top and blue jeans. He pulled a pair of reading glasses down from his head and swiped at something on his phone, squinting.

"Excuse me, miss, but is there a wi-fi password?"

I caught Sissy's face when she turned around. Her eyes were big. "Wi-fi? Oh no. No, we don't."

"Ah. I'm not getting a signal, it seems."

"Well. You can drive up to the PennDOT gravel pit on 18. That's usually high up enough to get a call out. Or Centennial Hill, in the graveyard. We're a little behind the times out here." She made up an ice water and pointed that I should bring it to him, and sucked her teeth like he was asking an awful lot.

Mr. Vanderjohn was still looking over the laminated menu, although I don't know why, because it was basically just a list of toppings you could get on a hoagie, or not. He ordered a chef salad with dressing on the side, so I knew he was about to be disappointed. The salads at Pecjak's were just hoagie guts with white confetti lettuce and no bread. Beneath the menu he had a stack of hot pink flyers. I recognized Jude's face, even though the image was blown out. It was a school portrait. She didn't look anything like the picture from the news, I mean, she was wearing a turtleneck and a suede vest. It said MISSING and REWARD in huge letters and there was a phone number at the bottom. He seemed to sense my eye lingering.

"What's your name?"

"Cindy Stoat."

"Aha, an old-fashioned name. I have one myself: Alistair. Perhaps you go to school with my daughter?" He pulled a flyer out from a tote bag at his feet and held it up next to his face. "This is her. I'm trying very hard to find her." He pointed at Jude's picture with his index finger. In the yearbook picture, Jude had a stiff smile, the kind you give to a person bothering you on the street.

"I don't really know her. But my brother was her boyfriend."

"Oh, of course—Stoat, Stoat. That's right. How is Virgil?"

"He's, um. I don't know." I was going to say Virgil was sad, except that wasn't exactly it. He was certain Jude had run away—and was it even running away when you were eighteen? He wished she had asked for help, but thought she could handle herself. "He's been helping her out. Bernadette."

"Virgil has always been very patient with her." He took a big breath and seemed to hold it in his chest. "Perhaps I'll see him. I'll be staying with Bernie a few days."

"I guess so," I said. Was I supposed to say something else? It felt like I should, but I had nothing for him. His eyes stayed warm for a moment, and then a more desperate thread ran through them.

"At school, was anybody—were there any—"

"Cindy, stop bothering the man! Get over here. I got a little work for you to do." She rolled her eyes like Mr. Vanderjohn was being ridiculous.

Sissy gave me a wet rag to wipe on the shelves, so I had to go all over the store and couldn't watch him, except I did see his eyebrows go up when Sissy put the salad down in front of him. He ate quick after that, like something about his day had been decided. I heard him getting directions from Sissy to the post office in New Freeport, and Bell's Grocery in Hundred, and all the other places to leave a flyer. The bell chimed behind him, and I felt for a moment unspeakably sad that he had to go around by himself with his flyers.

He left behind a stack of them at the register. There was a fifty-thousand-dollar reward for information leading to the whereabouts of Judith Vanderjohn of Deep Valley, Pennsylvania. It said to call the Guardian Angel Foundation Clearinghouse Hotline with tips. I had only heard about that amount of money on a game show. It seemed pretend, like Jet Skis or a brand-new car. I had about walked out the door before Sissy reminded me about the bag of sandwiches and cottage cheeses expired by a day and like that, and she let me pick out a candy bar but made me promise I would only eat it after I had ate a real thing.

"Can you believe it?" she said. "Wi-fi password. Huh. I didn't even know you could get internet on an Obama phone. Just not fancy enough, are we, Cindy? Nobody ever gave me a damn thing, that's for sure. I never needed a handout." I folded up the flyer and put it in my back pocket when she wasn't looking. I don't know why I was sneaking. I wasn't stealing it. It was there for anyone to take, even me.

The plastic bag cut down into my hands and I stopped a few times along the road to let the blood back into my fingers, which turned yellow-white. When the trucks went by, I listened for the last moment when I could hear them. At some point, it was washed out of the air and it was just me listening to my head's echoes. I could always tell when one was coming, the growl shifting up the gravel like thunder or a rumor, or someone about to shout.

A black car stopped in the mud. There was no place to pull over. The grass went right up to the road, and it was tall since Virgil never wanted to mow it after mowing other people's yards all day. There was a man inside with rain on his leather coat collar. The car looked steamed from the inside. He couldn't see me. There were vines. The dogs tasted the air after him. They didn't have names, so I called them both You, privately, in my head. But I called them Black You and Blond You so I could tell them apart.

The man came walking back a few minutes later. His curly hairs looked like they had been sewn in with a thick needle and his face was all putty. He came right up to the door and tried to see inside. Clinton was asleep on the couch. I shook his legs, and he swung out a hand that looked white like a blind fish leaping at me. The dogs were shivering. They wound around the man's feet and left paw skids on his khaki pants.

"Hi there," he said when Clinton got to the door. "I'm just here to talk about something. I'm from the high school."

Clinton folded down his sweatpants. They had come right up over his belly and he looked like a stuffed doll with seams in the middle. There wasn't any need but he turned on a flashlight and swam it over the man's shoes, up and down his thick legs.

"Hi there. I'm looking for Cindy Stoat. Does she live here? You the head of the household?" He had a folder of papers and he was licking a fingertip to get into them.

"Nome," Clinton said. "I'm not in charge of anything."

"Can I come in?"

"Better not. Power's out."

"Is this 288 Wildman Run Road? I need to speak with Donna Stoat. Is she your momma?" The drops from the man's brow were making dark blisters on the sheet.

"She ain't here."

"Ah, OK. Can you tell me when she'll be back? I got a number here, but your phone's out."

"Couldn't say. When she's coming back. The power's out, like I said."

The man stepped back from the door to sight the house, as if he might discover me hanging out a window or waving from the roof. Somehow I knew I had to hide from him. I had been watching from under the windowsill, where I could see up into his big poky nose holes.

"You'd be Clinton, is that right?"

"Whatever." Clinton had a high voice. Something had happened to his throat when his age started changing, and he got caught in this terrible middle place. Sometimes I could hear boulders squeaking against each other when he spoke. He sounded like a girl. There was something soft and foul about his voice, though I hardly ever noticed unless he was speaking to a stranger.

"Listen. We both know you're past school age. I'm not coming for you. But Cindy flunked ninth grade this year on bad attendance. Do you know about that?"

Clinton knew all about that. He was the one who went out to wave on the school bus when I stayed in bed. He was the one who told me I had fevers from being delicate, although I usually felt just fine. It was in the eyes, he said, which is why he could tell and I couldn't.

Actually, I liked school sometimes. I liked the classes where I didn't have to talk. I liked when we read about older worlds because I could imagine myself a lean little life of carrying wheat stalks and seeing demons and sleeping every night with rushes over my head. And I liked reading. Something happened to me where the words trailed off to the side and instead I saw the movie in my mind of whatever the words said. It was like walking into deep snow. Just at once, gone everywhere and the trees parsing themselves out of shadow, then shadow again. At home I had only one book. It was the folk tales of China. Mr. Loughman had given it to me in the third grade. I had to handle it very nicely because the pages were yellow at the edges and would snap off if I opened it too wide. Demons came out of the sea. In one story, a girl got a peach pit stuck to her forehead, and when it fell away she was marked ugly and made fun of. I tried to stick peach pits to my forehead after that. I don't know what I thought would happen, even if it had worked.

Clinton hated school, and never finished. He got beat up a lot, I don't remember why. He said it was OK that I felt sick sometimes. He said sometimes sick is something somebody else can see on you, and it sneaks up and you don't know that you're acting weird. Clinton always told me when I was acting weird, but it was news to me. When I stayed home, we watched TV together. When the power got shut off, we started running it off the generator, a squat clanking thing we moved from room to room. It was so loud you had to turn the TV to max, but I liked the static washing through what people said on the screen.

"I don't know much, sir, to be honest with you," Clinton said. He let a big spit fall out of his face onto the man's shoe. It stretched out a glittering moment before it fell.

"Look, someone's gotta sign this." He held out a packet where some of the words I could see were in bold letters. "She's gonna have to repeat the grade or go to summer school."

"Oh sure," Clinton said. "I'll drive her there myself! In my limousine!" He held the pen cap in his teeth while he signed.

"OK," the man said.

"I'll pick her up, too. In my dune buggy! Shit. We'll ride a white horse."

"OK, thank you," he said, and turned to go back in the rain. Clinton followed a few slack paces behind to make sure the man got all the way into his car and got it in gear and everything. The dogs rushed the fence as the car sped up away from us, and Clinton went out in the rain with them and pet them and wrestled them down till they were sickly excited.

"Yes, yes, babies," he said, smushing their faces. "Murder, murder. Kill, kill."

The responding officer, so I heard from Kayla, took a long time to understand what he had been told. He thought Kayla was the missing girl's sister. Bernadette would not let him in the house at first. She insisted he hand over his badge for her inspection through a slit in the screen door. According to Kayla, she brought out a spike of quartz on a thread and dangled it over the lump until the pendulum began to inscribe a clockwise course. Bernadette squinted at him, but let him in.

Kayla had to show Bernadette photographs from the wedding to prove to her it had already happened. She had pictures, too, from the campsite. Here they all were crushed in together with half their teeth showing in their smiles in front of the gorge at the lookout point. The flash had flared B.D.'s eyes into animal darts. In one picture, Jude stood behind the fire giving the middle finger to the camera. It was an unkind picture of her, from a bad angle, but the time stamp was true. In another, one of the girls was mooning the camera, her head cracked around to see Jude's reaction, Jude laughing and shielding her eyes.

"Isn't that something," Bernadette had said when Kayla pointed out the date in yellow numerals in the picture's corner. But her voice was vacant, the kind of thing you say when you don't quite understand the person you're talking to.

"Yes, this was two weeks ago, Mrs. Satterwhite," Kayla said.

"So you mean to tell me the girls already went on the camping trip," Bernadette said. Mondo was sitting at her feet and she chugged the loose skin on his back while he made a low, tense huff.

"Ma'am, this girl here says she was on the trip with your daughter."

"You—" She looked at Kayla, sitting in a small wedge of the overstuffed couch with her bony knees almost vibrating in front of her. "You're Marlon Whipkey's girl."

"Yes," Kayla said.

Bernadette stared into her hands and looked up between Kayla and the officer.

"Why don't I get us all a gin and tonic?" she asked. "Hot enough today."

"I'm afraid I need you to file a report, ma'am," the officer said.

"A report! Why would I do that?"

"Your daughter."

"Whatever she's done, I'm sure it's nothing an apology won't fix. Shoplifting, right? She paid them back for the lipsticks. I'll see that she never does it again. Just a moment. I'll get her down here—"

"Ma'am—"

"She's missing, Mrs. Satterwhite! She's probably dead. She's missing for two weeks. She's dead."

Bernadette looked into her hands and tilted the sterling ring on her thumb. "I know what it is. She's camping. At Coopers Rock, with her friends." In distress, Kayla pulled her hair down from its ponytail and racked it up again. Her nose was blotchy. The sun moved out from its mountains of cloud. Bernadette looked between the officer and the girl again, possibly making some calculation, then laid her index finger across her lip.

"You're Marlon Whipkey's girl, isn't that right?" she asked.

Everyone wanted to know: And where was Virgil on the night in question? Well, we had been in the VFW kitchen making coffee and like that for the wedding reception, of course. But it didn't stop anyone from wondering, and it didn't stop the detectives from asking him a lot of questions about his relationship with Jude. Jude and Virgil fought and broke up all the time, which had been true. Even I didn't always know for sure what went on between them.

People had always especially enjoyed gossiping about Jude and Virgil. They had been quite the couple. She would wear his Carhartt. He took her to homecoming, even though we Stoats do not, as a rule, attend dances. They were an infamous pair since he was a senior and she was just fourteen, unlikely and showy together like actors filmed by an invisible camera everywhere they went. As a private joke, they called each other Marilou and Cletus, and would discourse in the halls like high-toned rustic gentry. Jude wrote Virgil's name on the straps of her backpack in Wite-Out pen. Virgil defaced the back wall of the choir room with glow-in-the-dark paint. It matched the white cinder blocks when the lights were on but spelled out MARILOU IS EVERYWHERE in green capital letters when the lights were off. I have no idea what it meant between them, although it remains to me the most beautiful piece of art ever made.

Why, Cletus, if you aren't just the dandiest piece of pie I've ever seen.

Why, Marilou, if I could trouble you to sniff your wrist—

It was sick, how adorable they were.

Sometimes they parked at the calvary crosses on Centennial Hill to play the radio and listen to each other's heartbeats, and look out at the hills that rolled like the backs of tremendous dragons. Jude romanced the idea of elsewhere: Coeur d'Alene, Lansing, Laramie, Greenwood, Rolla. Why not work in a diner by a highway? When Virgil pointed out that those places were probably going to be just as much raggedy back-assed nonsense as Greene County, she said it didn't matter to her. Sometimes other places sound good just because they aren't here, and Virgil missed the whole point of feeling that way. This was the reason they'd broken up for good, I think. He had no curiosity about what it would look like to paste his life into another run of hills somewhere else, use a different kind of hot sauce, call crawdads something different. Virgil was of the opinion that this is the only life, and heaven is yours if you're determined to live in it. I won't pretend I know how Jude felt, but it always made me furious when he said such stuff around me.

But, Cletus, if I stay here, I'm afraid I might drown.

What do you mean, Marilou? I would never let such a thing happen to you, sweetness.

I'm already underwater. You don't even know.

I don't see any water.

That's the problem, all right.

VI

When Jude disappeared, it became clear that practically no one had any awareness of her mother's condition. Jude's friends, it turned out, had not been inside the house for years. Bernadette Satterwhite was not especially befriended in the community, except among the other artists and burnouts who had migrated to the area in a great wave at the end of the seventies. They had moved in on the cheap acreage in an approximation of something radical and dreamy. They would live off the land, away from what Bernadette called the murderous and ever-humming instructions of capitalism. So great was the influx that there had even been, at one time, a commune called the Whole in the Universe at one of the former farmhouses, somewhere in Ned or Spraggs or Rutan, although nobody could remember where.

After a decade or two, many of them blew off to more favorable cultural climates. I guess they hoped rural tedium would be a little more poetic, and not so much long winters of the snow chanting its death wish upon you. Those who stuck around picked up enough grit and crud and survival skills that they often could not be told apart from the rest of us, who were bent into catastrophe postures by poverty, black lung, heroin, WIC vouchers, fluoride, Miller Time, a caustic species of aloneness, perfectly well-intentioned social workers, postindustrial blight, single-A football, pepperoni rolls, and things like that. These things burned and bent the outsiders, too, the longer they hung around.

But Bernadette retained much of her singular presence. The kids along our bus route had called her a witch—to her face, which made her hoot with delight. There was a rumor she had come to Greene County naked on horseback, although only some very unreliable types would swear to it. Still, it seemed likely enough. Once, she had subbed for the art teacher at the school, telling the seventh graders that flaws in artistry were really just portals for the sacred to enter, which inspired a graffiti of poorly executed wangs and coo holes on the drawing tables. Sometimes she worked crystal healing at the sandwich stand inside Sissy Pecjak's gas station, right there in the particleboard booths scrubbed down to a foggy finish. You could pay her with half a hoagie or a few beers and she would lay the warm rocks where the hurts had collected in the body. It felt nice. It was mostly harmless, although Tamra Metheny and Dory Gitch and some other wives took a dim view of the practice.

Like all people who are proud of their grit, Bernadette's was mostly an act. She was born in Dallas, for godsakes. She had attended the Hockaday School, whatever that is. Before Alistair, she had briefly married the son of an aluminum magnate, when, as she said, "It seemed there might be some decent painting light left in Majorca and no other way to get at it." Yet she emphasized any opinion or false flaw that would make her seem like a simple country girl. She would rattle off her old grandmomma's skillet corn bread recipe at the mildest encouragement, even while she filled her shopping buggy with artichoke hearts and pomegranate juice and other things we all knew were high-tone.

Gradually, though, Bernadette stopped laying crystals and tried to master other industries. She bought a small herd of dairy goats off Creekmurs. She stopped wearing belly shirts. She was driving a pickup, like everyone did, and had worked on her fences. It seemed to most people she was getting some sense, and they were sweet to her about the trouble she took in finally courting it. She was really in over her head with the goats in particular. She showed up at the feed store with baffling questions—did the boy goat really have to pee on himself? Could she bathe the does in the tub, and if so, how was she supposed to get them up the stairs? But generally, the less people saw of her, the more they presumed she was setting her life to rights and walking finally down the middle of the road instead of hosting troupes of so-called puppet artists, instead of dowsing for a river to the underworld or hitting shamelessly on the UPS man.

Besides, her girl was liked at school. Jude had nice manners at sleepovers. She folded her blanket in the morning and helped make pancakes. She complimented the flower beds or whatever. Her mom couldn't be all heathen, people reasoned—but nobody thought for a moment those nice manners might be Alistair's doing, which, of course, they were.

In time, Bernadette's goat operation got to be pretty decent. She bought a Kiko bull from Preston County and linebred it with the Creekmurs' Alpines. The kids were a beautiful marshy gray run through with strands of amber, and white blazes on their rumps and faces. Occasionally, an FFA boy whose prize baby had gone sick with something killing—white muscle disease, milk fever, listeriosis from eating moldy hay—would buy a goat from her the night before the Jacktown Fair livestock competition. Bernadette's goats showed to great acclaim.

And so she was tolerated for quite a while. She could turn a friendly joke with the boys who loaded round bales into her barn. She kept to her own. She'd wave, without looking, to anyone driving by, her long skirt sweeping behind as she trudged.

But then, just the year before Jude went missing, Bernadette had leased a big parcel of gas rights. Her land was a stretch between two smaller plots that would support a well only if they were connected. Her neighbors on either side had gotten into the market too early and signed over for small royalties, but Bernadette drove the price up. This didn't endear her to anyone, of course. The people who got bad deals blamed her, even though all she had done was hold out. Everybody blamed her for the sulfur stink or the heavy trucks that chewed up the roads. Once the well went in, the air all around it tasted a little like freezer burn. When a whole truck of fracking liquid spilled out in the bend by the

Brant place, the gas company brought dozens of moon men in white suits to clean it up. Somebody had started leaving dead fish on Bernadette's porch—although I couldn't tell if it was a symbolic environmental thing or just intended to stink.

Something changed in the house—all of Jude's friends said so. Money is bad luck for dreamy people. And Bernadette had already been wealthy by Greene County standards, but now she had fuck-you money. Fuck-you money meant yes to all wants. Yes to sherry and yes to gin. Bernadette bought herself a Ducati she didn't even know how to ride, a white leather jacket for Jude. She bought tables made of black marble and capes of green velvet and enameled flowers that did nothing, just nothing at all. Any goodwill she had built up over the last ten years was over, just like that.

The day we first heard about Jude going missing, Virgil went down to Bernadette's as soon as we had unloaded the mowers. He stayed till dark and went back the next morning. I didn't understand at first why. It seemed nice enough, and Virgil did things like that. He brought big cans of coffee and bags of paper plates to people who had just buried family, or split wood when someone was in the hospital. But every day, every day, he was at Bernadette's and I couldn't imagine what all there was to do.

Once I saw the inside of the house, I didn't wonder anymore.

Bernadette had not been all that extravagant before, but suddenly she found necessary the velvet paintings and jars of fish teeth and fancy ashtrays where two storks held your cigarettes over the impossible calm of their silver and unrippled lake. She bought up Ormus gold, chaga mushrooms, and seminars on tape for the vibrational being stranded in a body. And whole lineages of Peruvian amethyst, whose advice she sought on financial matters. Eventually, she claimed she would open a consignment boutique. Lofting this idea allowed her to buy and keep whatever she wanted, even though she soon branched out to sad-eyed stuffed animals and balding rabbit-fur bombers and other inelegant junks, which began collecting in drifts around the doorways, crawling into the center of each room. By the time I lived with her, it was a funny thing. You'd drink Crystal Light from a gold-leafed Turkish teacup and eat hot dog soup at the prow of a mahogany table, with Bernadette blasting *Rigoletto* in the next room, picking mealworms from the oats.

And so it made sense that Jude had been acting strange before her disappearance. Amber and Kayla knew something was going on beyond the usual middle-distance stares on the school bus. Jude had threatened more than once to run away to her father's house in Rochester. She had applied early decision to a tiny liberal arts college in Vermont where the phone lines were troubled and unreliable, where snows sank the campus in a blind gloom for more than half the year. She had not even gone to the prom, and it wasn't because no one had asked. She had stopped listening to music. Something important in the middle of her life had gone still, or left her entirely, even though her mother was right there. It is a wonder to me what other people can miss in a life. It was so much easier to call Jude moody and teenage. And sensitive. And different. And all kinds of things like that.

Virgil came home from Bernadette's one day with a load of newspapers and two plastic grocery bags of weeds. It was almost dark already. It was a few weeks or so after we heard about Jude. He had sent Clinton and me to mow the Jollytown baseball diamond ourselves, so our moods were not so high that day. The newspapers were for following Jude's case. The weeds, apparently, were for us to eat.

"It's fiddleheads. Bernie showed me how to scavenge them," he said. "I figured we hadn't had anything green in a while." Clinton and I trudged into the kitchen after him, because apparently they had to be cleaned and such. Clinton especially found the whole thing ridiculous.

"Like fucking fun am I going to eat this," Clinton said. "This is some wild hillbilly shit."

"Come on," Virgil said.

"She's just not a right woman. You couldn't pay me enough to give her a foot rub or whatever you're up to."

"I ain't rubbing her feet, Jesus."

"There is nothing you can do for people like that."

"People like what?" Virgil asked, but I think we all knew what kind Clinton meant. It was not easy to pick scales from fiddleheads. Clinton cussed low and righteous over it. Virgil must have told her about our mother being gone, because she had also sent him home that day with all these weird cans of things, stewed mussels and artichoke hearts and fava beans, which we had certainly not heard the first thing about. Clinton meant people with gas money. People who heard you were starving and gave you cans of stillborn vegetables and a bag of weeds to eat. People like that.

It was a proper disaster. They had grabbed up some nettles, which apparently Bernadette meant for us to eat, too, but we were throwing them in a bag on the floor instead. We yipped whenever we got stung on a handful of those by mistake. Virgil kept his eyes on his hands. He brushed a piece of hair back and left a streak of mud on his forehead, a permanent shadow. Clinton saw it, and winked at me. But I let the wink go. I didn't catch it with my face. I imagined it shooting past my shoulder, the wink, miles and miles and light fast so it would soon be all the way out in space.

"Tough cookie," he said to me, and then turned back to Virgil. "Look, I get it. She's sucking you off."

"Jackass. I don't know. She's always helped me out. She was good to me."

"I'll *bet*."

"What's she like," I said.

They both jumped their shoulders. Sometimes I startled them without at all meaning to. I think they forgot I was listening.

Later on, when the kitchen light turned yellow, I felt a horrible wash of drowse start up from my feet. It crushed my lungs, my guts. It was taking me on inch by inch, and I fought it hard, but the lights in the kitchen were so bright they went into spots. I knew, like you know in a dream, that I should not fall asleep. But I also knew, with awful dream certainty, that I would fall asleep anyway, and the dread dripped against the back of my throat, but it was sweet and sweet and sweet. I had been eating too much candy because we had some. And that was what I did when we had some, which is why we didn't have some often, but Clinton and I had thumbed it to Pecjak's that day, to get some black and red gumdrops for me specially. Not even any good, if you want to know. When I bit through them, I could see the grooves from how my teeth came in wrong. My teeth looked fluffy at the edges, like a cartoon cloud. And they left slick lines down through each gumdrop, which got caught in my snaggles, and I hated the black ones so much I couldn't eat them at all unless I spaced them out, black red, black red. Coming to the end of each one, I was just doused in sadness.

"She's like a witch in a storybook, sweetness."

"No way," I said.

"Oh yes," Virgil said. "She is a real honest witch. You can tell because she eats mice and wipes her boogers on the wall."

"Naw," I said.

"Don't believe me? I saw her bury a Bible once."

"You got dirt on your face," I told him.

"That's to keep me safe," he said. "So I will know to follow where the lord leads me."

"That don't make any sense," Clinton said. "You fucking cocksucker."

And then Virgil began whistling a gospel, which is what he did when he wanted us both to hate him. *What wondrous love is this, O my soul, O my soul.*

Clinton pried a black licorice loose from the bag on my lap and caught it in his back teeth, his head cocked back like a bird's. "I do believe she's a witch, though. I'll give you that."

"I bet she doesn't wipe her boogers on the wall," I said. "I bet that's not real."

"Witches are women who do just as they please, so long as what they please is right in the ways of the earth," Virgil said. They sounded like borrowed words, and I felt a cold fluid rise in my spine because I saw these were her words, the words of the witch, and they had reached through space and now they were in my ears and mind.

"If you wanted to stay really safe, you wouldn't go hang around a witch," I said. But he didn't answer me.

I was too old to believe in witches. Or what I should say: I was old enough to know that I couldn't go around confessing that I wanted to be one. There were witches in my book, and they were not usually bad, just particular. Or they could do strange things that made people afraid. They became, somehow, the same thing to me, that Jude had disappeared and her mother was a witch. I yearned myself toward them like a root striking down through a boulder. I was deadly, but just from tireless wanting. We boiled the fiddleheads in salted water. Clinton made retchy sounds while he swallowed. But I was determined to like them. I felt them bring a strength into my body. Maybe I was brave, even. Afterward, Virgil sat under the moon. Clinton watched the nightly lottery draw. When neither of them was watching, I went back to the kitchen and drank the fern boil water straight from the saucepan, all its green depth, and announced myself as a secret apprentice.

When it got around that Bernadette had filled up her house with infomercial junk, many were scandalized, and by this I mean delighted. Some had been waiting for her fall quite a long time, especially after the gas deal. It's hard to like a libertine if you can't remember the last time a rule has ever been bent for you, and where I come from, just about every woman is jacketed in iron about what's real and expected and possible, and what you had better look like, and how nice you had better sound. Bernadette had lived so loose it was like she just shrugged off bad luck entirely, and so when it finally found her, it was the kind of thing people discussed with savor and joy. That was the carnival feeling at Pecjak's, the day we first heard the news. I know it sounds cruel, but no less do people rejoice in that way. If trouble found Bernadette at last, it meant there was a law. It meant nature would assert its levels. My mother would have crowed over Bernadette's wet brain if she'd been there to witness it.

My mother didn't care for any of the back-to-the-landers, but she began her disdain for Bernadette in earnest when Jude and Virgil were dating. For one, Virgil never brought Jude by our house, and for another, he ate dinner at Bernadette's every night he could manage. He'd come home talking about tarot cards and how the death card is really about transformation, and how the divine feminine is ever alive. And he stunk like myrrh, and he started using new words and knowing of mysterious customs, such as the *New York Times* Sunday crossword puzzle. He was talking about college, psychology or something like that. But what really did it was Bernadette would let him sleep over, in the same bed as Jude, and make them lemon pancakes in the morning like that was a sane, average thing to do for teenage lovers. That just wasn't real in my mother's view. She called Jude a jezebel and a jiggaboo. She feared for Virgil's idiocy.

My mother was the kind who would be very offended if you called her a racist. She talked about it all sideways at best. The most you could get out of her was: I don't approve. And she trusted she did not need to speak any further on the subject. As, generally, she did not. Whoever she was talking to usually knew exactly what she meant. Her disapproval met in the air with the disapproval of whoever she was talking to, and the two silent moods married and had their own life, in the air all over us, in the water, in the mind. That was the trick to it, never having to say what you actually meant. Nothing is real if you don't have to say it.

The paper ran at least a daily sidebar on Jude's disappearance. Most people had noticed Jude's absence at the wedding already, and had long settled down into gossipful reckoning by the time the actual investigation started. Melda McConaughey told anyone who would listen that Jude was dead, that she, Melda, could feel it, and could see the flashes of the underworld through a portal into Jude's mind: limbs heavy with fruit, tossing in a black wind. Oh, Melda.

Or possibly some people didn't even think on it so kindly, if that could be considered kindly. For some people, Jude had gotten herself into whatever trouble had swallowed her up. Believers of this notion spoke in sweet and pitying ways. They said "drugs." And there was that baggie of weed, after all, as they were pleased to point out, never mind that Jude only had it because, as Kayla confessed, the rest of them were too chicken to buy an eighth themselves. What people meant was Jude was a brown girl, and that bad things happen for a reason. Clinton was one of these. Suddenly he had a memory of Jude as a drug dealer. She sold people pills out of the library, he said, and had once offered him a stamp bag which he had the good sense and fine character to decline. "She had a pager and everything," he'd tell anyone. Anyone would listen. Never mind nobody on earth had used a pager in fifteen years, except on reruns of *Law & Order*, Clinton's favorite show.

And what bad luck of hers, to turn eighteen just a month before. Even the sentimental machinery that found lost children wouldn't work on her. With babies, it was all flyers and AMBER Alerts scrolling across the digital bank displays. With Jude, it was that JanSport with the vodka bottle in it. The *Post-Gazette*'s advice maven, Dotti Eisengart, even wrote an Op-Ed bemoaning the lagging investigation. Miss Vanderjohn was no delinquent, she claimed, unlike so many young people in the rural areas who "landed askance of god's laws." But the local police force was already small and aggrieved. A scolding didn't incline anybody to look any harder, and neither did the implication that the rest of us died primarily of our own trashiness.

And anyway, what could the police do? It fell to the family of the missing to make a show that would keep the news cameras hovering around. Alistair had his billboards and his endless five-minute interviews with morning-news human-interest anchors, but Bernadette was in another world altogether. And, to be honest, although no one cares to admit it, I think we just weren't looking that hard. The year before, a sixteen-year-old white girl disappeared from a sleepover in Star City, West Virginia, and you could almost feel the hum of panic in the search party. The school district canceled classes for a week so students could aid in searching on foot. In Jude's case, nobody knew where to search and it was summer vacation anyway—but that wasn't the reason nobody looked for her.

The girls from the camping trip finally admitted that Jude might have run away after all, which Virgil had been claiming all along. It was something of a theme with Jude. She endured Greene County the way someone might endure a community service sentence. When the detectives examined Jude's room and determined from the empty hangers that about two full duffels of clothes were missing, it seemed possible. These had not been found in her car at the towing station, and neither the bartender nor the fentanyl addicts had mentioned anything about the girl they had seen carrying luggage, but possibly Jude had sent them ahead. Possibly she had meant to leave without fanfare, even though this seemed not to square with the events of that day.

Alistair Vanderjohn knew nothing of Jude's plans, apart from having invited her to visit awhile in Rochester on her way out to Vermont. He had last spoken with her the day she had gone missing—Jude had called him on her cell phone to keep her company while she waited for the tow truck, and had told him the whole drama while she skipped stones in the crick behind Burchinal's. Naturally she was furious at first, but by the time she hung up, the whole thing seemed funny to her and she didn't sound troubled to him. He did not know whether she had gotten into the tow truck, or some other vehicle. Their closing was brief. She cut him off to say her ride was there, and then the muffled, windy good-bye, and then nothing.

Some held it suspicious that Alistair had not known of his own daughter's disappearance. The two were apparently quite close; Jude usually called him three or four nights a week, and wouldn't he become somewhat concerned to hear nothing? Yet it didn't trouble him. He said she sometimes got caught up in a mood or enthusiasm like any teenager, and he did not care to read much into it. As to her plans of running away, he had never taken them seriously. "Living in an isolated place can be quite painful. And wonderful, of course. Bernadette made clear that she wished to raise Jude in nature, and I see the wisdom in that. But it has not been easy for her. Not at all. And we do talk about that often." And what, exactly, was that supposed to mean, everyone wanted very much to know. But it was clear enough: Alistair also knew how hungry she was to be someplace different, hungry enough to leave without a word of good-bye.

Besides all that, Bernadette had apparently been drinking quite a lot. She kept a gas station travel mug near all the time, and whatever was in it was red. She tried to be very casual, but if you paid attention, you could see how she followed it always with her eyes. Very gradually, she had stopped going out on her own. Every few months Alistair brought her around to the doctor, the feed store, the library, and wherever else, but the trips got more difficult as her memory shrank away. I don't know if he ever tried to sober her up. I always figured they split up because of her drinking, but I guess he still couldn't resist trying to help her, no matter how impossible it became. She had apparently advanced on the shores of not this world completely. The doctors said it could be a brain tumor, cancer, anything that made her forget, but the drinking had some part in it, and was also likely why she refused all treatment. By the time I came around, her forgetting had worked itself in a loop. She could remember all the words to "The Charge of the Light Brigade" and the names of all the Paul Newman movies, and she could even quote passages of *Being and Time*, split right from her memory. But she couldn't remember whether the oven was on, if the eggs had just been set to boil or were cooked into chalk, and because she was also proud and afraid, she would never admit that she'd meant to do otherwise. We ate a lot of raw eggs. Once she had cracked them, what did it matter? She claimed to feel wonderful. She had not been to the doctor in twenty years, which she credited to cold showers and aromatherapy and shadow work. And truly, her health was undamaged otherwise, apart from high blood pressure and a problem she described as "glass in the knee."

But the mind was another matter. Bernadette believed that an angel was sleeping in her bed. She believed there had been a series of ravagings in the tristate area. She believed her Tiffany silver stolen, and accused the last person she had seen that day of taking it. Sometimes she accused others: Jimmy Carter, Ricardo Montalban, Doris Day. Jude she sometimes accused also. Jude was hiding from her. She found it most childish.

She believed a quality of sunlight was capable of healing welts on the body, although she would not let on where the welts had come from. They were a rude pink shine on her arms and thighs. She believed in signs. She believed it was late May, even as the days were swelling to the full-throated height of summer. She sunbathed naked by her mailbox, apparently, until Virgil or another neighbor came along to wrap her in a blanket. She always had her travel mug nearby.

Bernadette said she had seen bears roam the property line, churning through the fizz of heather and forsythia scrub. This was not unusual, taken on its own. Somebody saw a bear every summer, although often, once they had sobered, they demoted it to catamount or coyote. Bernadette reinforced her fence lines with woven wire and hot strands. She worried for the safety of her goats. She kept a shotgun by the front door and vowed to get the bastard. She laid traps desultory and literal: a plate of honey sandwiches on a stump in the side yard. When Alistair tried to help, she apparently confessed that she felt simply awful: She had, after all, invited the bears, and communed with one sexually, and so she knew she had brought the whole miserable trouble upon herself, as usual.

Bernadette believed she had a constantly praying heart. She believed nothing bad would come to her. She believed she was still young in the eye of the universe. She believed the smell from her sex was a reliable perfume and dabbed it here and there. She was a witch, and she believed she could call hellhounds down to wail in the valley and do as she bid. She believed it unnecessary to consult any calendars. She believed all cops had been criminals in the last world.

She did not believe that Jude was gone. Hiding, she always called it. Detective Torboli interviewed her often. I usually watched from the top of the stairs when he came around. The top of his head glowed like the white inside a polished gem. Bernadette always wore something special and baked banana bread—he was handsome, and I think she must have liked the attention, aside from his dreary questions. She wasn't worried about Jude, not one slice, she told the detective, while they gazed over their coffees. Jude had developed the most astonishing skill—she could hide inside an object, locked up entirely. She could hide inside her old black-frame glasses. She could hide in the trunk of a tree. But she always—Bernadette shrugged as she said it—came back.

VII

It was a handsome Saturday. It had rained for a week but the mud was getting dried out and all the drains in the house smelled like living green mud. The ladybugs were millions. They got in my breakfast and down my shirt, they died in waves. I wasn't to do much chores around the house, but Clinton had me sweep them up with my hand onto a piece of notebook paper and throw them out in the yard where we threw things.

Virgil had not been home at all for a few days. Once the detective was able to convince Bernadette that her daughter was gone, she went mad with grief. Virgil worried she'd cut herself up or drown in the bathtub, so he stayed around the clock. And Clinton didn't say about it, so I didn't say about it, and the green fur was coming back up in the divots, tender and new and shivering from all the effort. I was to want myself a little nice time, maybe. The sky looked blue with an echo in it, like it was a bowl really, and I could feel that the earth was truly round, other teachings no matter.

The fish fry was happening already and I was anxious to get going. I was afraid Clinton had forgot. The fish fry they did only two times a year and I loved it because the air shimmered up and we didn't eat much hot food, and I could watch all these grown people and see what they did and how they spoke to each other. I had a mad curiosity about people, even though they frightened me. It was nice, when something big was going on, that I could slip around and not be noticed, and get my fill of what they looked like, what people's knees looked like with the fattish dimples riding on top, how they looked at each other when they liked each other. I liked the things about how people put their clothes together. I liked their white leather purses and the lines around their mouths where the lipstick was darker and ragged. By now, of course, I know I was so curious because I was primarily curious about myself. I could see my outlines in what I wasn't that other people were. I had pink cowboy boots with a curtain of scallop fringe along the sides. Sometimes I saw the scoop of how I walked along in a grown-up woman, and I realized that my hips were able to switch a way I couldn't have done before. It was exciting on some days. Other days it made a sad soup in my throat.

I knew the fish fry was that day because the calendar we had, the only one, was the one the volunteer fire department handed around with pictures of red unbelievable and fast cars. Clinton had, for once, taken off his glasses while he slept and the way his face was pale, without the usual red furrows, frightened me. I put my fingers in his mouth. His tongue had gone dry in patches. The other parts were silt velvet.

Clinton swung a hand at me and missed.

"Goddamn, chickie. What? What?" He squinted around to smell me.

"It's the fish fry," I said. He wouldn't move, so I got his billfold out from the pants that hung jacklegged on the back of the chair and took out five dollars.

"Oh, all right. You gonna be a thief now."

I shook my head.

"Gonna be a little sneak thief." He talked like it was a game we were going to play.

I shook my head again and put a hand on the door, because I didn't like the sound of what he was saying.

And then I was on the floor. My tooth hit through my lip. Clinton had come across the room at me and pulled himself down on both of us, collapsed us both. His fingers dug into my ribs like a tickle, and like a tickle I laughed. I couldn't help it. I didn't want to laugh. My neck froze in a hard line.

"I got a thief right here," he said hot in the hair behind my ear. "I caught one."

Other times when Clinton held me down, I bit him. I had once bit a shred off of his neck. *Shaving*, he told Mom. But I couldn't find a place to bite with my nose caving up against the floorboards, lacquer caramel dog hair down in the cracks. He was vined around me and had my arms pinned back.

The laugh that came out of me was a round, wobbling thing. It was a balloon I could set on fire and send out over the county to give somebody an idea. It was a shiver. I hated it and tried to scream through it but it sounded like laughing still, no matter what I did. He dug his fingers down and plucked at me.

Something winched up in my belly cut itself loose. My front was warm. It was piss. It hissed under me hard. Clinton paused, moved one of his hands under me to feel the floor.

"Oh, god," he said. "What you have to do that for?"

I was wearing the pink jean shorts that were my favorite. The dark part looked like a lake's edges, but then the piss fled out and blurred into a circle. Clinton hauled himself off me to see and I rolled, like that, all of one moment, out from under him and out the door and through the dog run where the mud was still slick from their always bothering it and mixing it in with their turds all day and the last snow in the shades leaving crusts around them like craters, just holes that went down somewhere, and I ran down the road while the sun put its flat part along my back like a good thing.

I had his five dollars in my hand running behind me. In the wind my running made it like a flag. When I turned around there was the rushing sound of the breath I took and nothing else, except birds and a wind in the branches looking thicker by the day, so leafed they were exhausting to see because so pretty.

A little harder I heard a stream going nearby like a *dime-dime* sound, the sound of peas dropping in a tin bowl and rolling. The back of my shorts was messed. Pee went dry on my legs and then it started to leave like a dust from where my legs rubbed together. I was happy to have the grit coming off but I wanted to be clean.

The crick came up around me when I sat in it. It was cold like needles and my blood rang away to warm me up. My shoes filled. The water lifted my feet a touch here and there. It felt good to let my legs go do that and get heavy.

I decided to die in the wilderness. I saw that if I could sit down in the leaves I'd be warm a little while, although I partway knew this went counter to my suicide. I practiced arranging the face of death upon me, how I would be discovered. And reached up to twine my hair around on the ground a bit more prettily. I did this kind of thing often. I would imagine being watched in my sleep and pillow my head on prayer hands so whoever could see me would think: What an angel on earth. I did the same thing in the leaf bed, except elevated to permanence. When I closed my eyes, I saw fat black grapes, a green exploding fountain, a landscape I could never share with anyone. Daylight was like a white block of air that moved around the earth suffocating everything but the ants and the ladybugs, the things so small that their shells were like bunkers. Ticks suck on everything because nothing can get inside them. I thought I might feel one crawl my scalp, and swatted but of course I couldn't tell. I would be cold when they found me. The blue would brush in on my lips. And *why, why, why* is what everyone would cry at my funeral, all except my mother, because she'd know. She'd know it was because she abandoned us. And her knowing would be a darkness that would never leave her. A cloud of blackbirds broke and turned above me, and I knew her shame would be like that. So perfect in its intelligence that it could toss it in the air, wheeling and fluid.

I closed my eyes and tried to see what I imagined Jude was seeing, from inside the castle of her being gone. The dark in my head was buzzing and green. It was air all around me and in my mind. Anywhere else. I kept trying to imagine a bad oblivion, and my mind wouldn't let me. There: So I was jealous of her. That was the problem. Take me instead, I begged the air. Maybe the shimmer that took her was still hungry.

It got dark like the life ticking out of something. The clouds were whipping past the sun. The sky got rounder, and there were soft spots higher up where I knew it was being space and that's all. My stomach hurt. I hadn't eaten. I peeled myself up with my cold muscles hammering against each other.

I would have gone back that minute, but I couldn't figure out where I was, and I was furious at myself. I walked along fast and low like a beetle though I had a stitch drawn up through my ribs. I kept turning to look behind me, to see if there would be a certain angle that I recognized, a familiar way the trees flushed up in the sky.

I stopped in a place where an oak had grown a little dent on its side and slid myself in so it pressed my arms hard against my sides. Would it be better for him to find me or would it be better for him to not?

In some stories, the person who is lost gets more lost because they're looking, the people looking for them only find the places where they were. I followed the crick until it went out of sight, and then I walked back to see if I could find the same spot I had been in. I wasn't sure. The ground was uneven all over. The trees moved against each other while I walked like a strip of repeating wallpaper. I listened hard for road sounds, and I didn't hear any. Only ten or so cars went by our place every day, on average. I knew this because I counted them every day. I had a little bookkeeping ledger I found in the closet where I marked the day and date and each car and its time and color.

I saw his hat first. A figure was coming toward me along the brambles that were all a green dust. "Cindy, Cindy. Come on," it said. It was Virgil.

I looked around for the five dollars. I thought I had been holding it the whole time, but it was gone. I thought of the five dollars sheltering in a hidden root tent, shuddering in the wind alone like that. It made me cry. I cried to think of anything being alone, even if it could not draw a breath. Virgil let me up over a little bit of scree, and then we were on a tractor path that turned this way and that way, and off of it was the gravel piece that went down to our mailbox on the main road. I had not even been very well lost. We were home hardly any time later. He did not ask me what had gotten into me. He didn't tell me what I should have done instead.

Clinton was standing by the door when we got there. Inside it was so dark it was flat, just whatever path where I walked that kept making itself. Virgil steered my shoulders away to the bathroom. He had me wait outside while he got the hot water there, and then he stood outside while I got in. He said he would stand outside until I was done and make it so nobody would bother me. So I sat a little while watching the sad scummy white my skin turned in the water. My hairs floated in that slow, darting way. I was very surprised. It cost too much to make so much hot water for a bath, and we almost never did.

"She was nuts. Grade-A crazy," Clinton was saying. "We wrestled around, she was out the door. That's all it was." They were talking outside, trying to whisper.

"I heard enough about it," Virgil said. "I'm done."

VIII

The day after I had run away, I decided to not talk, maybe never again.

But running away made everything worse, of course. It made plain all the things that I tried not to think about. I worked very hard not to think about Clinton, but there wasn't much else to think about since it was the early summer when every day had eight or nine eras to it, and no hope of going to school. I could smell him stooping around the house. With Virgil down the road every day, it left it so Clinton and I were once again watching the noon lottery draw while the day shot down on us from high up. I got so sick of Clinton I would go stand in the exact opposite part of the house from him. Or if he was in the middle of the house, I would crawl under the porch with the dogs, where the dirt was silky.

So I had decided something. I got up early before Virgil left to go to Bernadette's. It was still dark and I sat in the passenger seat with my stolen candy and my magazines and read by the light of the dome lamp. I had never been allowed to sit in the cab before, so it was quite shocking to me that I had done this. I was reading the names of lipsticks in a catalog and thinking about what I would like to do wearing each one. I would like to be in a city. I would like to stand on top of a skyscraper. I would like to eat a little poached fish, whatever that was, in the company of a man with smoke leaking out of his mouth. Coral. Coral. I said the word and half saw these things. I trailed my fingernails over my arms and my mind fled.

I think I scared Virgil. He jumped back when he saw me there saying coral and coral and dusky berry.

"Bunny, you go back in the house."

"No," I said. Had I ever said it before? We don't know.

"I'll come home for lunch today and check on you. How about that?"

"No." I said it with my whole body. I said it like a witch would say it. "I'm coming with you. I'm not staying here with him."

"OK," he said, and sighed. "I'll take you to Bernie's. But you can't go upstairs. Not for anything. Not at all. You get me?" When he started up the truck, I glowed in my victory.

We got down off of the ridge in stages. Something felt scary about being in the little room of the truck. The way Virgil took the turns, sometimes we slid out into the middle of the road. I had never noticed before, but he wasn't a very good driver. I was always in the pickup bed on my back watching the leaves wash over, looking up at the white breaks where the sky fell through. Virgil sat forward and jigged the wheel back and forth with little jerks, with his thumbs pointing right up in the air.

The road bottomed out and we went around a turn past my old elementary school. It looked like it had shrunk down since I remembered. There was a trailer attached to the side by a rotting wooden ramp. Some saplings were vowing themselves up into the air in the middle of the baseball diamond.

Bernadette's house up close was bleaker than it looked from the road. The windows had tails of black grit up their centers like they'd been scorched, and a part of the apron porch fell away from the house. Or possibly I had been thinking so hard of Jude, witches, fern spells, that just seeing the house in front of me felt like something watery from the silent and dead place where my mind liked to go. The side yard was eaten down to the clay by a pack of goats penned in with wire wrapped around cinder blocks, and more cinder blocks had been stacked up into angular islands here and there. A goat stood on each one, seven that I could see. They were healthy, tremendously beautiful goats. They stood still as if I wasn't watching them, and maybe I would just go away.

We stood awhile looking into the dark screen door. A stack of newspapers under the porch swing had molded into a column with a green fume along the edges, and there were trays of orange fruits with the pits slashed out of them drying in the open air, like shrunken hearts.

"Bernie!"

Virgil slipped his hand through a slit in the screen and snapped the latch up, and we walked into the gray dark. The rooms were big and fell away from the sunlight even without the curtains. There was a heat like something carried around in a pocket a long time with too much human use to be any good. Virgil was already through to the kitchen. I put my hand on a chair back to find my way forward. It was warm to the touch, like it had a fever.

I had never seen so many things in a house before. I felt like the floor was about to roll away beneath me. There was only a little aisle between the grocery store circulars and plastic Santa statues and boxes of microwave bacon cookers. Trinkets and plastic bags went down in layers. Sometimes my foot crunched on a hidden thing and the sound was sick in my stomach. And everywhere was the evidence of superstition. An old much-faded poster taped to the back of the mudroom door showed the arrays of the *I Ching*, with grubby shadows where a hand had consulted, over and over, the ideograms. I could hardly see through the kitchen window, where the concrete mucilage tamped around the frame had been studded with crystals, railroad pennies, the little rigid birds from inside sand dollars. It was hard to look a long time at anything. Everything had the intelligence of objects handled much, the sparkle of that. Above the door the saints Anne, Bernadette, and Pio on their trading cards, Pittsburgh Pirate Dock Ellis on his, and AFL-CIO buttons dug into the soft wood. Tin stars. There was laundry, too, or clothing, at least, on everything in soft, saggy piles. It felt like walking through a melting gut. Spider plants, a scummed jug of Carlo Rossi, a toppled pair of riding boots with a sky-blue tempera stripe painted up the side. There were twin figures in a set of small boxes tacked up on the wall. I didn't even know that they were all ornamental salt-and-pepper shakers. I had certainly never heard of such a thing. They had stupid, inconsiderate faces. They didn't look like they were meant to be of any help. Virgil dropped down in front of the sink cabinet and got out a bucket and a scrubber. I picked up a mariachi and his girlfriend and wondered at the holes in the tops of their heads.

"We're going to get things cleaned up around here. Help me get all this picked up. But you got to be quiet, and you can't go upstairs."

I smiled because I had never seen him tidy a house.

Virgil was bagging all the obvious trash, but what was trash wasn't so obvious, except for the Sno Ball wrappers he was punching down into the garbage bag. He looked unnatural working inside. The way he bent over I saw he was getting some belly slub under his T-shirt, and his cheeks were full from focus. Maybe it was a look he shunned from his face, but he seemed younger. Or maybe it was the impossible task. I stone stared around at all of the junk. Embroidered pillowcases, a bowl of ash, white plastic poodle barrettes, slide projectors, hubcaps, baby blocks. One low table carried five statues of peacocks. What are you going to do about a thing like that? I arranged them so they were all pointing their heads together in the middle, then gave up and stirred them randomly around with my hand. I picked up the bowl of ash to help dump it out.

"Nuh-uh, wait, wait," he said. "That's probably for something."

"For?"

"I don't know. It looks important."

"It's burned-up garbage, Virgil."

"Trust me. Anything that looks like garbage is probably, like, her conjure shit."

"Oh, so like these?" I held up a Hostess Sno Ball with a bite pinched out of it, and a dizzy ant wandering its landscape.

"Fucking, fucking, I don't know. Just help me. Just try."

Sometimes I was actually a good cleaner. I knew how to feel the edges of things for invisible smut, and I liked how I could put part of my mind away from me in a high flat place and collect it later. I liked how after, my lower back felt tight, like a punch. The place had not been cleaned in a long time, and as I moved things around, even as quiet as possible, the dust foamed up into the light. It smelled very living, like the shade on a lake. And I felt very aware that this was the air that had slipped into Jude's lungs and mixed with her blood and become her. I could sort of understand why she might want to run away. The house felt heavy, like it could fall into the earth.

There were books everywhere, in stacks, slanted against each other up the stairs, and some facedown on the spine of the sofa. *Gone with the Wind*, *The Death of Ivan Ilyich*, and *Edible Appalachian Foraging Plants*. *Man and His Symbols*. They were all in the fussy plastic coats of library books. I looked in the endpapers and saw they had been due two Januarys ago, which delighted me.

The best thing about that first day was I found a nest of boogers on the wall next to the sofa. If that was true, I thought, the rest of the witch things Virgil had said must have also been real. I was going to scrape them off with my fingernail, but then I decided they might of course be an important magic thing, a piece of work, so I washed very carefully around them with chore water instead.

A stack of cereal boxes had toppled off the refrigerator. Each one, when I opened it, had about a mouthful of cereal so stale it hardly snapped in my mouth. I ripped out the bags and flattened the boxes. I found a bunch of plastic bags under the sink and started putting like with like. Under the sink, I found eight or so glass bottles with the labels ripped off. The air in them was hot and fat. I held one over my face and got a needle of it on my tongue. It felt alive somehow, like it was still fighting after I swallowed it, and right away I panicked that I must have poisoned myself. I couldn't hear Virgil anywhere in the house. I was about to yell for him that I had been poisoned but then saw that one bottle's label had fallen under the few at the back and it said Gilbey's Gin so I knew I wasn't going to die but also that I shouldn't tell him what I had done. Since Virgil was not a drinker, I thought it might upset him that I had tasted some.

I was standing tiptoe on a kitchen chair to wipe the dust off the molding that lined the kitchen and something in my guts switched. My lower back went hot and I felt in my face the cool lines of bile rising through my spit. I had to grab on to the wall and then the cabinets to get myself down. It was all too light in my head, but not in my legs, which were rotten of blood and held me stooped over a minute before I realized I was about to shit myself.

I didn't think to go outside and shit in the garden, although in retrospect it would have been the better idea. But the goats frightened me too much. They weren't afraid of me. Their eyes were yellow with square holes in the middle. I knew there wasn't a bathroom on the first floor because I had walked through all the rooms, not cleaning exactly but just seeing what was there, and I knew it was important not to go upstairs, but I did. I had to climb over boxes of naked baby dolls and tinsel and videotapes and light-up palm trees and plastic sandals. I choked up my steps as much as possible and skimmed my feet so the slats wouldn't groan.

An enormous exhaust fan stood at the top of the stairs with a long pull chain. It had been roaring like that forever. The sound made me think like a fly, like I was something to be sucked up into nowhere, although the breeze it made was a small thing.

I found the bathroom first of all. I undid my shorts and they hit the floor the same time as my shit filled the toilet. I also felt a beautiful relief. It felt so good to let the sick spill out of my body. My lower back felt dry and fine again, my sweat dried, and I wanted to sit there forever in wellness. There was a church newsletter in the stack of mail and magazines next to the toilet and I read a recipe for tuna noodle casserole with potato chips on top.

The knock was polite and hesitating.

"Is that you in there, honey?"

"Yes," I said. And panicked that I should have said nothing instead. But then, would she have come in to check on me? Where was Virgil? I had forgotten all about Virgil making me promise to stay downstairs. I wondered if she was maybe dangerous. I knew people could be bad news if they were sad enough. My shorts were still on the floor circling my feet.

"Do you need help?"

"No," I said. "I'm fine. Sorry. I didn't want to wake you up."

"You didn't, honey." And then: "Jude, honey. I didn't mean any of those mean things I said."

I didn't say anything at all. I weighed it out in pieces. The floors were pine painted clear. On the far wall a Metropolitan Museum poster of a silhouette flown flat across the sky with its heart thudding crudely. The afternoon must have been winding down because a stab of light flew into the room through the door crack. The doorknob was shuttling.

"What do you mean?" I asked. "What did you say?"

"Why are you hiding from me? Why are you hiding? Are you scared?" she was hissing. "I'm your mother. Why are you hiding?" There was more that she said, but I didn't hear it because I was going *oh shit oh shit oh shit.* Something was pounding on the doorjamb. It wasn't locked. But she was hitting her fist there and sobbing. The sound was a drowning thing. She breathed in big shaky gulps. She rasped like ripping a sheet of paper in half. "Baby, baby. Honey lamb. I am so sorry." And then her steps shunted off away. Floorboards sprang on the other side of the house, or maybe it was the bed. It sounded like she had thrown herself down on it. And then it was nothing.

I cleaned myself and put my shorts on again. They felt heavy and damp like they were made out of animal skins. I washed up for a long time because I didn't know, I was afraid she would be hiding to jump out and grab my throat. I even ran the bar of soap on my armpits and splashed water in them until my skin squeaked. When I left, the hallway was empty. The utility fan tolled on like an alien headache.

When Virgil finally came in the house and clapped his hands on his ribs to say he was done fetching for the day, my heart was still shuddering. All the sounds were leaping my pulse, so I had picked up a book to get my mind to go elsewhere. I was reading *The Death of Ivan Ilyich*. I had flipped to the middle at random, where a woman wanted children so they were putting honey on her parts, which was so wild that I had forgotten I was sitting in the middle of a witch's house.

It's strange now to think about it, those first few days in the house before I met Bernadette. My memory is so full of what came later: her fussing, winding yarn around a cardboard guide to make pom-poms for our boots, for Mondo's collar, and eventually all the goats, or boiling down gingerroots when we both caught coughs from the damp, hanging the ginsengs that looked like fat little headless babies trussed at the feet. Or burning up cardboard boxes in the yard and stirring them around with a busted rake, just like my mother did, ashes and flake touching off on the wind. Probably she was sleeping it off that day, but I would know about that later.

When Virgil came down the stairs I realized he had changed clothes. They were perfect new. The pants were darker in lines across his legs where they had been folded on a shelf. He was putting something away into his pocket.

"You ready, then? What you got there?"

"Can I take this?" I asked him, holding the book's cover toward him. He squinted.

"You can't take things unless you ask. How about we'll ask next time."

"Can we ask now?"

"Leave it, Cindy. Put it down."

I stood up carefully, since I had already hid *Gone with the Wind* down the front of my shorts and I didn't want its line showing at my T-shirt. Even after how she'd scared me, I knew Bernadette wouldn't mind.

IX

There was a girl Clinton talked to on the computer. Her name was Shayna and she lived in Port Arthur, Texas. She called it a greasy old hole. She raked her hands through her hair, a repeating claw, and pulled out brown pieces of it and dropped them to the floor where I couldn't see.

I got stoned on watching her. The blue light bloated her face, or it was the camera. It looked wide though you could see her chin pointed out so she was healthy and not too fat, but that was the kind of thing a girl could fool you about by how she held her head, was what Clinton said. He had a lot of girlfriends in other places.

Shayna sounded like everybody I knew, ever. She didn't want to work at her job which was, when she did it, to sell soaps and lotions at a store in the mall. She had drawn eyes around her eyes with a purple pencil and she looked mutated from a mirror with frayed edges where she blended the skin-looking stuff in. I knew it because she did the makeup while she talked to Clinton. While she worked her brushes, another woman roamed up in her like shadows falling off of the sun.

Ever since our power had been shut off, Clinton ran the computer and the internet off of the generator, which meant I couldn't watch TV when he talked to Shayna. It was so loud I didn't know how they could hear each other at all, but maybe looking was the point. In the rest of the house it was dark and so quiet. Clinton would close the bedroom door as much as he could, but it had been painted over so many times that it hung off the floor by some inches, and wide of it there was a gap I could see through.

I started on the couch with my ledger in my lap. Sometimes I drew pictures of the cars that had gone by that day, except I added my embellishments: They were all on fire, they were all bucking over the moon, they all had eyeballs for wheels, and things like this. Other times, I drew castles made of crystals and tears, and big crying roses, and women wrapped around swords. As it got too dark to draw I waited to hear her voice snapping out of the speakers like electrified dust, and I would slide kind of down and over until I was basically on the floor and I could just see her running like blue TV light all over Clinton.

"I care about the way it gets written down," she would say. "I can't have them thinking I don't pay attention in case they want to overcharge me on something else by like a hundred dollars. I want them to know my name when I call." Shayna rehearsed a lot for the rest of life. There was always a revision of the things she would say at people.

"That's good," Clinton would say. It seemed really boring to be a boyfriend. I wanted to know when he would ever talk about anything that wasn't her paperwork.

She was shaping her mouth while she said all that so her words came out in blunt lumps. She dragged a dark brown pencil around her bottom lip and used a Q-tip to fuzz the edge in.

"God, what was I even saying? Sorry. I'm so fucking done. I have this hangover I can't get out from under."

"Are you going to work tonight?" he asked her.

"Yeah, a little," she said.

I knew somehow that they were talking about a different job that was not selling lotion at the mall. But I had not entirely figured it out. It was something like she liked it but didn't want to let on. I could tell she was making it sound more boo-hoo. And Clinton always asked. He always wanted to know.

Sometimes I got a funny feeling, like my skull was getting too tight, and I would pluck at my eyelids or press on the bridge of my nose to click the bones inside. I felt strange like that, watching Shayna, except I didn't fidget. There was a certain way, if I crossed my legs, that the seam of my shorts pressed against my privates and the feeling was a well but also a wave.

I sat up straight to push the tension better and my leg flung out to the side, the glint along the shin, I didn't know where the light was coming from and I thought I had better stop, I had better stop before they heard me but Shayna was hanging her head down and brushing the underside of her hair. She looked like some species of alien. I ran outside and stood in the dark. I didn't know what I was doing except totally. A car was coming. Its groan got higher as it washed closer and I saw the headlights start winking up through the branches. That kind of rain that falls through you from outer space, so light, was coming down and it was hot out. I stood up behind the fence and lifted my shirt as the car went by. I don't know what I hoped they would think or do about it. My belly underneath my shirt was blank and mottled and had red rasping all through it where the little bloods blushed on the hot night full of chap. Greatness! The air rang around me and I dropped down behind the fence just after the car passed so they wouldn't see me, and I'd be a ghost, and they'd wonder.

One day, Shayna was real, by which I mean she was really in our house. Clinton had gone to town for food and new tires for one of the mowers, so I didn't pay any special attention when I heard the truck idling down to nothing in the shed across the dirt road where we kept it. But I heard her voice instantly. It was high, like his, but she sounded happy. She was carrying a box of groceries with a big purse hiked up on her shoulder and sunglasses on top of her head. She turned and laughed at whatever Clinton said.

At first I presumed she must be someone famous because I knew I had seen her face before and she was skinny, famous skinny, and her arms were a hard, dark color. I had only seen her in the blue computer light before, while she did her makeup and shook out her hair and chuckled over the camera. I could tell I was staring at her, which made me more shy. Clinton looked grim, like he was holding something heavy from the corners of his mouth. Her arms moved in bright forms. She looked like she was the only real thing, like the grass and tree dust were just a backdrop. I would learn that she created this effect by applying careful layers of fake tan spray and shimmering dust from a purple tube. She put it on every day and stood like an X in the bathroom while it settled on her skin. She would let me sit on the toilet and flip through her magazines while she did this.

Shayna had brought all of her clothes for the visit in her huge purse.

It was white snakeskin with pink and blue streaks. She had a lot of clothes in there, but they were all small things like shorts and halter tops, or tubes that stretched out when she pulled them down from her armpits and turned out to be whole dresses, aqua and orange and silver lamé.

Clinton seemed unhappy. I couldn't tell if he had known she was coming. The two of them would disappear into Mom's bedroom for the afternoon, and I could tell they were having sex by how quiet they were. I mean, they still made sounds, but the sounds they were trying not to make were louder. Tentative and shuddering things. I imagined a chrysalis the size of the whole room shifting and tearing with a dull plastic light at its middle. Although of course I tried not to linger near the door because I didn't want them to catch me when they came out.

Shayna was my immediate best friend because she brought a stack of magazines. I loved magazines. I loved looking at people. I never got to see anyone. It was different from reading my catalogs. All of mine were for things like Sears. The people didn't look like they even had belly buttons. I had never put on makeup before and I didn't know that I would like how it looked on me, but I started to wonder. I looked at the magazines whenever I could.

The women in the magazines had vivid faces. Sometimes they looked hurt or lonely, but gorgeous. Maybe I was used to pictures of women who seemed happy to see me, women who seemed to be saying: Holy crow it's snowing look how happy we are about it in snowsuits from $49.95! I knew that wasn't real. But sometimes I caught myself smiling back at happy pictures, or at the TV when the story was about something good happening, like a woman finding her lost dog or a girl getting laser surgery and throwing away her glasses forever. That's how stupid I was.

These women were not like that. Nothing was actually happening to them but they looked perfect. No, it was something else. They looked like they knew things. They knew that they looked perfect, and it seemed like they knew I was looking at them. In whatever second the photographer had taken the picture, I felt, they were looking right at a future where I was scraping the dust off the bottom of my feet from the filthy kitchen so I could tuck them up under me while I read, by which I mean I looked at the pictures, and the summer heat swelled up blue in the far-off hills which I could see walking off so slowly that they seemed not to move at all.

One day, I asked Shayna to do my makeup for me, and she laughed.

"Oh, sweet thing, I couldn't do that. What you got is called a fresh face, you know."

But I didn't. My face looked like a thing made of dough. I had lots of freckles that touched almost, and dusty moles that stood out from my neck. At fourteen I had decided I was ready to be a woman. I hated how much I was looking for in the mirror. You could tell by my eyes that I wanted to see someone else there inside my face.

At first, she would only give me a little bit of light lipstick and some mascara. I sat on the toilet and she crouched before me, one knee up. I felt funny when I looked at myself. That sick feeling, and something winching up in my stomach. The mascara made me look like I had more eye than usual in my head, and they were already too big. The lipstick made me look like I had been feeding at the wound of a killed thing, a wolf. Shayna's armpits smelled like onions, but it wasn't gross. It made me hungry. She was wearing a peach shirt tied up so you could see her stomach.

"What about like this?" I showed her my favorite picture from the magazine. It was from a set where all the models made evacuated shapes against the mirror wall of a skyscraper. The one I liked, she had light brown skin and her hair was pulled up from her face as a globe, almost like a head directly above her own head. Her eyes were dark and blue-dark and glittering. She wore a gold chain with a rectangle attached by the corners, very small, and her mouth was wet and shining.

"Well, we'll wash it off before Clinton sees it, OK?" How did she know we had to hide it from Clinton? I hadn't thought about it, but she was right, of course. Clinton was the one who got upset about my outfits and called my cutoff shorts "racy." Shayna winked, as I recall. Would that be all it really took to win me over? Who's there? Who else is moving the scenery? Is this a chewing gum commercial? Are you my mother?

But as I've said, I smiled at nice things happening to people on television, so it was possibly as easy as that.

Shayna opened the curtains that covered the small, high-up windows so she could see in natural light. Up in the faraway corners I could see daddy longlegs dead and folded up into diamond shapes in places. I was to keep my eyes closed, and the brushes skimmed down over me in a way that I thought about moth wings batting against a screen. I could feel her breath, sour and cool, moving over the bridge of my nose. She was only a year older than Clinton, but I would have believed she was thirty-five rather than nineteen. Her face had attained certain angles I associated with minivans and sun freckles and Kmart jewelry. She and Clinton drank canned margaritas all day, slow and civil. As she worked, she told me to look up and down sometimes, and sometimes she swore a little when I blinked and ruined the line she was trying to draw under my eyes.

"There's a girl who died from around here," I said. I was trying to impress her. I felt strange that we weren't talking. "I mean, she probably died. Nobody knows for sure."

"Oh yeah," Shayna said. "I know some dead girls."

"She disappeared after a camping trip. Like, vanished."

"That happens. Or maybe she wanted to disappear," Shayna said. "I knew a girl who everybody thought was dead, but she had just got married." I couldn't believe how easily she had thrown over the most dramatic story I knew.

It felt like nothing was happening, and I wondered that maybe she was tricking me, running empty brushes all over my face to please me and she had no intention of really making me look different. She blew under my eyes. Some parts she blended with a fingertip and her long nail scratched under my eyebrow but I didn't move. All her attention was like a heat moving over my face. I was afraid that I would start sweating, even. I was somewhat offended that Shayna didn't even care to talk about Jude. That was my prize, the best morsel I had to trade with.

When she let me look in the mirror, I was a creature of some lovely pain. I could have been somebody else. There was new gravity in my eyes, which sank and sank me down against my own edges, except now my edges were everywhere and my body shifted to make space for them. My bones were aluminum. I could not talk to anyone without being terrified as myself, but the things I could imagine this face saying, using words I didn't even know, I had to touch my lips to make sure I wasn't saying all of these wild things out loud. Then Shayna would be afraid of me, if she knew about my metal bones. For the first time in my life, I realized that I could get up and walk out of that house and never come back.

"Wow, huh?" she said.

I said wow.

And when Clinton and Virgil came in the house swearing at each other for fun with pollen luffing up out of their hair and I heard the chairs stumble around in the kitchen, Shayna said *shit, shit*. She ran a pad of paper towels under the sink and gave it to me to clean myself up with. She shut the door a little too loud. A little too hard, she demanded Clinton take her somewhere for once so she could get a cold drink and eat a real dinner.

It hurt to take the makeup off. I didn't know how to do it. My face was rubbed red under my eyes and smudges of black stayed around my temples like ink and soot. Why had I been crying, Virgil wanted to know when I came out of the bathroom a long time later. The house was empty. Clinton and Shayna had already gone off. Virgil was dealing himself a hand of solitaire. But I had not been crying. I had not, and I told him.

Shayna had been staying with us for what felt like a long time, although I figured out later it had only been about a week. Every day, I stole a lipstick or mascara. Soon I had a little kit which I hid under my pillow. I put some on every day and dared anyone to say how grown I looked. It's insane, how you can have a whole new face and nobody talks about it. But I did look older. I could feel it.

Around that time, Virgil started letting me walk down to Bernadette's by myself and clean the whole day alone. He picked me up at five each day and took me to Burns Delite for ice cream. I felt the apology in it, but I didn't know what it was for. The police were interviewing him, of course, although I didn't know that at the time. It was quicker for me to walk, anyway, and I didn't think too hard because it felt so good to get out of the house and away from Clinton. Down the steep side from our back porch I could make it in five minutes through the woods, and feel my lipstick warm from the sun and feel the heat of grass growing and the drowsy tumbling bees. Every morning Virgil reminded me not to go upstairs, not for anything, and not to wake Bernadette up. I had not seen or heard her since the day we talked through the bathroom door.

I knew where to slip my hand through the tear in the screen like he did, and got adjusted to the heat and smells and the house's ways. I would sit in a pile of silk kimonos, pink sateen dressing gowns that caught on my hangnails, shift around the salt shakers and touch her brass and crystal arrangements in a way that was possibly spiritual, an experiment. It was the beginning of ritual. Usually my feelings rushed in over me like water. They fit so close I didn't notice them, or I thought it was just bad light pouring down, and the bad light had an itch for me no matter what I did. But when I wore Bernadette's strange striped pajamas over my jean shorts or balanced her tongueless copper bells on the backs of my hands, I don't know. I found a distance. I found a perch where I could watch the moments tolling down. They were desperate and beautiful and stark.

I didn't seem to make much progress cleaning. No matter how many bags of garbage I hauled outside for Virgil to take, the next day, I found the spot I had cleared again crushed in with promotional tote bags and jars of buttons and things like this. I wondered if Bernadette came downstairs when I left and pulled more junk out of the closets to cover the bald spot I had made in the carpet.

One day, I was cleaning the oven. It was still hours before Virgil would pick me up. I got a piece of newspaper folded up under me so I could kneel in front of the oven. It was the worst mess in the house. Someone had been shoving things in there to clean up in a hurry. It was the same trash, the standard trash, except also plates with food rinds on them, and big undisturbed clusters of mold that were airy as dandelion moons. The oven itself was scalded black and dusts of dog and dry skin had fuzzed in the thin strip on the floor before it where the wood gave way to red linoleum. It felt wet on my face when I opened the oven door. A few times I had meant to deal with the oven and just stopped dead at the thought, but I began and I began by doing just one thing, throwing away one thing by one thing, and happily I made my mind to throw out the goddamned whole thing. A trash bag swallowed it all like a feasting snake. Even the plates. When the oven was clean, it beamed back while I looked. I mean that I could see my face in it, but it also had acquired a kind of intelligence.

I hauled everything outside and ran my head under the spigot on the side of the house, sat on the concrete steps with a warm Coca-Cola and watched the goats. They watched me like I was an ocean, and might do anything to them. Summer was going to stop soon. The dust was starting to stick to the catalpa trees. They were sick of standing up in the sun. The air kept on thick but I knew better than to think it would be hot forever. The days would stop. It was plain.

I had the idea that the goats might accept me and come to think of me as a goat if I sat there long enough. This was the kind of weird thought I had all the time then. I thought I could change things in the world by thinking them, so I thought about them all the time. And the first goat would approach me and lick my hand, and the others would come. I was not like anybody else, and they would see this. They would circle me and tell me things and show me how they climbed along the leanest little pickings of slate on a hill. Fearless.

I had found a pack of Camels under a half-done crossword puzzle with a book of matches tucked into the cellophane, and they were sailing me out to a new idea. It was a dry day, the first when the wind had gotten chill and real like something slipping up from all of the basements. I knew just how to light a cigarette from watching Virgil, although nobody in my family was supposed to smoke or do anything technically sinning, and yet we didn't do much of anything else. The cigarette tasted like wood, and spit welled up in my cheeks. The nearest goat blinked in the cloud I drew onto it but remained essentially uncomplaining. I liked my life. It gathered itself in an invisible fist around me and the air shimmered like something had slipped over it perfectly see-thru and tricky. I could name them, I realized, the goats, and feed them apples until they liked me, and if they didn't like me, I could hardly care. Even I could see how dreadful my life was, but something about its ragged elements had combined in a way that was refreshing and funny and so much my own that I could eat it up and never be gotten at.

This is how to live, I realized. To set something on fire. That is what is required.

I don't know where I get this trash. So unoriginal! Such a menacing thing, so ordinary. It powers everything. In every switch and ion there is a girl smoking her first idiot cigarette under a corrugated tin roof and etching a difference into the air. Try to find a jukebox free of the sentiment. Try to find a waterfall that isn't made of this. You'll die looking, I promise. The search party will quit and go home.

I was still stoned on the luxury of my thought when I stood to go back inside. I was starting to hold my hand out to the doorknob but found Bernadette in the way, watching me. My arm burned where she grabbed it. We flew to the couch where she laid me out over her lap, belly down. This all happened in a rush. She pulled my shorts down as far as they could go and thrashed at me with something like a black leather flyswatter. It didn't really hurt. I was too big, and she couldn't find the right angle to swat me hard, but my forehead ground into the tweed cushion and I tried to bring my arms around so I could roll off and away.

"Where have you been? That's all I need, seriously, you go off like that I'm just, it's over. Dammit. Dammit dammit dammit."

I tried to scream, but my throat was all air.

"Now, oh yes. Now we're scared, oh yes."

I pulled myself up and righted my shorts. She was breathing hard. I saw she was sweating all over but wanted to say more.

"I'm sorry," I said. My mouth was a clenched line and I could hardly get the words out.

To get to the door, I would have to rush past the couch where she could no doubt reach me. She had strong fingertips. They dug at the back of my shirt. She had pulled me back and held one elbow. She slapped at my ear. It would have hurt worse if it landed but her aim was wrong.

She was wearing a purple kimono over a men's undershirt and boxers. Her stomach was fish white like mine, and her legs and arms were so skinny. She stared me down with her breath ticking. Then her eyes dropped, and she cleaned her lip corners with a triangle of tongue.

"Honey," she said. "I'm sorry. I did it again, didn't I? Let me make you a sandwich."

She steered us into the kitchen. "I've been thinking we should really get ourselves out of here on a trip," she said, scouring the fridge for cheese and butter. On the table, grocery store circulars were spread open like the bottom of a birdcage. "Someplace with a good coast, where they have those lodge motels. What am I thinking? Oregon, I suppose. But I need to see the water, Jude. I'll be dead soon. My god how I've missed you."

I knew I wasn't the one she missed. And I should have been scared. But I don't think anyone had ever said such a nice thing in my direction, with the voice meaning it also. The tears started way back in my head and I pressed my eyes closed to stop them. I missed my mom. I missed how she would take our hands and polka us around the kitchen when we were in bad moods and didn't even want cheered up. "This ain't no party, this ain't no disco, / This ain't no fooling around."

Bernadette hadn't noticed my silence. It took her no effort to keep up the conversation all by herself. She had a nice way of moving around the kitchen without needing to look at anything.

"I know you hate it when I talk about death, but there it is. It's the one thing we're never incorrect to fear. Your godmother, I mean, that woman would love to tell you that heaven is the afterlife. Of course she wants you to think that her prayers will keep me alive until you find a provider. It's just that I ask you"—she was shaving curls of butter from the block with an eye held squinted—"to consider the source."

Mondo nudged himself under my feet so my heels sat on his spine. I tensed my thighs to hold them up. There was a speedy rush to everything she was saying, how it wrapped around me.

"I think we really ought to get some rhubarb in the ground this year. Well, of course. I'm always full of regrets! At this time of year, it's just about dead anyway. I have your aunt Shirley's recipe for that tart you like. It's almost good if you double the sugar. She thinks we all have diabetes, or will any day now." She tipped the sandwich onto a plate. A teardrop of old grease clouded the side. "You're awfully quiet today, sweetie. Is something the matter?" I had already bitten the edges of the sandwich and had tented my mouth to let out the steam. I had no idea how long it had been since I last had hot food.

"Not really," I said. "This is good."

The smile that broke out from her face for this was a shining thing. I found I didn't want her to put it away. She propped her head up on her wrist. Light touched the top of her hair again and I could see it was red under the dark.

"I just hope you'll tell me when it's boys. Really, I do. I know a thing or two about all that."

"Ugh," I said.

"Oh, it's coming. You can't doubt it. And I'll tell you this: We have always been very lucky in love, the women of our extraction."

I'll tell you a secret: Acting is nothing. Acting is what you have to call it later, to seem remorseful, after you've said how you wished and done how you wished and blew up your breath into the shapes that you liked. So I used this strange moment to try saying the truth.

"OK," I said. "There's a boy. But I hate him."

"Maybe you really love him?"

"No, I hate him. I don't want him to touch me."

"What does he do?"

"He, like, tickles. And other stuff."

"Yuck," Bernadette said. "Ticklers are the worst. Cowards! No ticklers for Jude. Absolutely not," she said. She scolded the lit match she held against her cigarette, and waved it to death with a slice of her wrist. "The only solution, I'm afraid, is a murdering."

I swallowed a sharp bit of crust. Was she serious?

"Oh yes, we will shoot him. Right in the jelly of the eye!" I laughed out of alarm, more of a bark. Then we laughed at that. And she threw back her head like she was drinking hidden rain, beautiful. Beautiful. I had never laughed before, I'm sure.

"I'll kill him, I'll drown him in the ocean. We'll fill him up with juice until he turns purple and his stomach falls out." I was still laughing. My blood rang. It felt so good to say a thing like that, even though maybe what I said was a bit too strange.

Then the sun went behind a cloud and we were sitting in just the glare from the window. The radio hit a pocket of garble with the grainy high holy of the gospel station trying to push out from under the arpeggio, saxophone, bells. Bernadette studied the cuticles of her thumbs and had drawn her lips into a line. I was still eating the other half of the sandwich.

"Who are you," she said.

"I—"

"No. You just tell me who the fuck you are this minute."

"I'm Virgil's sister. I'm here to clean."

"I don't know any Virgil."

"He mows. He bales the hay. He's tall," I said hopelessly.

"You have to leave," she said.

"He's coming to get me at five."

"I'm from Texas, and I know the law. I can *shoot* you."

"Well," I said. "This isn't Texas. It's Pennsylvania." For some reason, that reminded her of Jude, and her face caved in.

"You killed her! My baby, oh god. It was you!"

"I don't know where Jude is, I promise! I promise. I don't even know her except from school."

"How do you know her name? How dare you. My baby! She's dead."

I was up out the door with Bernadette after me, again. Except this time she wasn't trying to grab me. Her spit flatted itself on the back of my leg. Another spit hit my T-shirt. When I turned, she had dropped to her knees. Her mouth swung wide with no air or sound coming out. I heaved myself up the hills, scrabbling my hands over roots to hold where it was too vertical, the leaves too slippy, they came away in big swipes under my heels and the blood would just pop my head open. I wished to be a tick and stick myself to the skin of the world and just live on what it fed me without fighting, and that is how I got up the hill, up onto our ridge spine, where Clinton was throwing a knife at a rotted stump and Virgil was nowhere around.

Virgil took me back to Bernadette's the next day. He said it was all fine, and she got confused on him sometimes, too. Sometimes she thought Virgil was Rock Hudson, sometimes her childhood love Bobby Bickham. It was the drinking. He said he was going to explain to her properly who I was, and fix the sink in case she didn't believe him, or in any case he said it was good to have a clear reason to be in her house when she got confused. She got most confused at sunup and sundown, he said, so we went once the light was calling down unbroken in the middle of the dry morning.

We knew something was wrong right away—Bernadette was in the living room, sat on the floor with her legs in a V and her head cricked back at a painful angle on the couch. Smoke poured out of the oven.

Virgil got down on the floor by her to slap her loose jaw some, just light taps, and she came back up to the air with her eyes struggling. They spun like the cord that kept them in place had been cut. He waved me into the kitchen. The stove blared at me. It had been on all night ticking and grumbling. She had torn open a bread bag from the end that wasn't supposed to open and the two pieces she had tried to toast were scorched so thorough that they fell away in black dust when I touched them.

Bernadette had one of the bottles I had found under the sink clamped into her hand and I couldn't get it loose. It smacked out against my arms while we carried her up the stairs and into the bathroom. Virgil hoisted the shower curtain to pin it around the rod and we lowered her against the front where rust stains wept down from the fixtures. The ring around the drain was jungle color, down all the way inside it. Clear water charged down while Virgil turned her head back and forth on her neck in the cold stream. The bottle rang against the tub so loud I was afraid somebody would come and arrest us.

When she yelled, it wasn't anything that matched with words, but sharp so I knew she was hunting back from the hidden place her mind had been, and Virgil turned off the water so we could get her up. She could step over the edge of the tub but needed carrying to the bedroom. It smelled strange and strict in there, strong and leathery. Her clothes swarmed from the closet and up onto the bed. There was only a little lip by the pillow where the covers had been pulled back. She slept under a pile of coats, like everyone had just left a party and run out into the snow.

Virgil sat her upright and turned to get something from the closet to put around her shoulders, which is when I noticed that her chest was out. Both her titties had slipped up out of the stretch-neck T-shirt, which had got wrapped around her waist. When I turned away, she fell flat from the bed onto her face and my nerves sprang out all against each other. When she sat up, the blood was guttering out of her one nostril, and she was laughing.

"Oh my god," she said. "I've really done it this time."

I held out a sock for her to catch up the blood.

"Aren't you sweet," she said. "But I'm fine, fine, fine. Wow. Wow." We left her there, saying that on her side.

We put the splayed furniture back into the divots in the living room rug. I threw the burned bread dust out into the yard and a goat helped itself to the black grass.

In the basement, Virgil showed me where to look for her bottles. Alistair had shown him, I guess. I don't know why any of us thought it would help since she always got more, but maybe it was enough to feel like we tried. She had a few tricky places where he checked first—the underside of a workbench furred in undersea dust, a shelf behind the plank stairs. I thought it was crazy when he took the lid off the cistern, but he hauled up a triple-bagged bundle tied with twine and lashed around with fishing line so you couldn't see the thin wire of it, at the lip of it, gone down and down into the darkness. He moved on to an ancient walnut hutch crowded with canned grapes. The cans were dusty but trailed with dark finger sweeps from where he had looked other times. He came out with another bottle of gin.

He poured out the bottles, ripped the labels down the middle and peeled them from the seam of glue along the back. I didn't want to touch them because I knew they had a kind of power. Our mother had quit drinking when we were babies. Her method was to starve and get beautiful, buy lotto scratchers, read the Bible, scrape my hair up into these crinkle French braids that made me scream since she had to comb them out until they were right and the blood bounced under the skin of my skull. She sewed all of our clothes. She put Virgil in pageants. She made him a Superman costume that looked like the real, perfect thing.

Virgil bagged the empties, and had me put them in the truck bed nooked against the back wall where they wouldn't roll. The handles bit down through my fingers and being in the sun made me hard tired, like I had just pulled my new self from an egg. When I went back inside, the sun had burned my eyes so Virgil looked like a red-and-green swarm.

"What it is," he said, "is she gets upset when she remembers that Jude is actually gone. Listen, I need you to check every day and pour out all the bottles, OK? Check all the places I showed you."

"OK."

"She helped me out," he said. "You know. When Mom wasn't around." But I didn't wonder why Virgil wanted to help. I wanted to help, too. I thought Bernadette was wonderful, if a little scary.

"She thought I was Jude. A few times."

Virgil thought about it. "Maybe that's the best way, actually."

"To do what?"

"Just do things to keep her off of it, you know? And keep her from burning down the damn house. Maybe if she thinks you're Jude, she won't have to drink so much."

On the way back up to our ridge, he pulled over by a gravel bay where the turn went wide. The engine ran. He hooked both bags around his fingers and tossed them down where the hill fell away into jungle. I couldn't hear them roll, but they shook the vines. It looked, almost, like a creature was about to appear there.

The hair dye was my idea. Virgil had said I should keep Bernadette's mind off her troubles, after all. It was just an experiment. It was just for a little while, to make Bernadette feel better. It was a kindness.

I wondered why she'd suddenly turned on me when we had just a moment earlier been peaceably eating sandwiches and planning Clinton's death. The only thing I could think was my hair had been wet, but when it dried blond, some important piece of the resemblance fled. That was the only way I could figure it. If I dyed my hair and found a spare of Jude's glasses, maybe I could keep Bernadette from thinking about her missing girl.

To be clear: This was nothing but delusion. I look nothing like Jude, even disregarding skin color. She had the tuned bones of someone nearly grown up, and her forearms were bladed with muscle. I was pudgy from eating and starving and Pepsi and salt. She was much taller than me, with wider eyes. My face was still round. And I had a way of standing around which indicated I would like to be pulled inside out and swiftly disappeared from the earth. Jude had another sort of way about her. People shut up when she raised her eyes to them. By this I mean: I was no brilliant actress, with no real disguise. Bernadette was in much worse shape than anyone knew.

Actually, Jude and I do have the same kind of low voice. We both sound like we've been smoking hard, longer than we've been alive. Virgil had even said so before. But that is the only resemblance I'll claim. It's no great struggle to trick someone who asks you if you want coffee, then pours you some, then asks again.

One day, I got Shayna to walk with me to Pecjak's to buy us some Popsicles. We had been watching *Dr. Phil* all day and our thoughts seemed unreal. While she was paying, I slipped down the aisle and put a box of black hair dye down my shorts. It was easy because Shayna was telling Sissy Pecjak about how to draw perfect eyebrows on a face.

"No," she said when I dumped it in her lap back at home.

"It's not for you. It's for me."

"You got the kind with no dimension to it. Blue tones'll make you look like an old tooth."

"I don't know nothing about tones."

"Yeah, clearly you don't. You sure? This shit'll make you look dead, I'm just saying." She sighed. I pulled her after me into the bathroom and sat on the closed commode.

The dye was cool. Something unlocked in my spine as she painted it on my skull. I felt like something had snapped right in my backbones for once. She piled the strips of my hair up in a do on my head like a curled swan. I got taller, I'll swear it, right then.

We didn't either of us have a watch or anything to tell how long to leave it setting, so she flatfooted into the kitchen and grabbed the clock, a sad cardboard thing, from the wall. Up close, the second hand shivered each time it ticked, which I had never noticed before.

"I'm bored," I said. "I want a Pepsi."

"You're gonna *be* a Pepsi." I loved it when she said things like that.

"What does that mean?"

"I don't know, my mother says it."

"What's she like?" I didn't know what a big question I had asked, because Shayna told me the whole story.

Shayna had apparently been working at the Bath & Body Works in

Port Arthur, but she was just a year out of high school and it wasn't enough money to live on her own, so she was paying rent to her mom to live in her teenage bedroom. She felt like if she was going to pay rent she could at least be someplace where she didn't have to pick up the second phone in the kitchen and hear about her aunts' knees and backs and pelvises. She seemed to live in a shell that wrapped around the house and the mall and the gas station, and which she couldn't quite figure out how to leave in a real way. Then again, everybody else had to live within the shell, and life was the shell. It didn't seem anybody was escaping. But then one of the other girls from the store was suddenly buying everybody smoothies and new purses and eating fifty-dollar all-day brunch and nobody could figure out where she was getting the money. She told Shayna she had a webcam show and people would watch her lie around in her underwear, and they tipped her extra for pulling down her bra or touching herself or dancing, and she had one regular who tipped her out what she'd make in a whole week of selling Lovely Dreamer body lotion for bringing the computer into the bathroom with her when she took a shit. So Shayna got all the lighting and equipment and made a profile called xVapeQueenx.

Shayna had no idea she would like it so much. But it was like stepping into a tall truck. It wasn't the usual bullshit, the way men would drive by her slow and make kissy sounds, say I can smell you from here and all that. Or it was exactly the usual bullshit, precisely the same, except with compensation. They were just names, DannyBoi87, TomKat, eddie_murderfag. They didn't have faces and they lived for her, and if anybody said a foul thing she could banish them from her personal chat room.

But also she learned things about them, almost by accident. DannyBoi87 was gone every few weeks for complicated intestinal surgeries that made him itch from the painkillers for weeks afterward. TomKat's sister was an infirm teenager who pissed her pants and failed out of school and needed his endless attention. eddie_murderfag liked to pull the double-grown hairs from his chest with tweezers and paid extra for Shayna to rub jelly and peanut butter on herself in the tub. Her regulars lived to gang up on the amateurs who sometimes dropped in to critique Shayna's thighs or talk hatefully. TomKat was a particularly attentive guardian, and he never pestered her to talk for free, and he never talked down to her, so she made him her enforcer. His devotion to his sister impressed her enormously. His life sounded hard, but he was resolved in decent cheer about everything. When they started talking off the clock, on Skype, it was her idea. She told him her real name. They started to plan shows together. It was TomKat's idea that she should set up the laptop next to the tub and demonstrate some other uses for Lovely Dreamer body lotion. They had a good thing going. TomKat was Clinton, of course.

Shayna's mother was a hospice nurse who worked long days, and Shayna did the show only when her mom was out of the house. The more elaborate her sessions got, the more she worried she'd get caught, so as added insurance, she leaned a two-by-four against the front door so if her mother came home unexpectedly, it would clatter over and act as an alarm.

But a terrible thing happened when it didn't work. Well, it did, but the two-by-four fell sideways and smashed a ceramic pig doorstop, and Shayna's mother assumed there was an intruder nearby, so she picked up the plank and stalked through the house with it. She heard the tub running. She heard her baby girl making noises. Anybody would break the door down. Anybody would bring the plank down on whoever was hurting her child, except Shayna's mom found only Shayna in the tub, drools of body wash glossing her tits and the laptop chiming for tips like pachinko, and the twitch in the muscle that registers shock was already thrumming, so it was impossible for her not to keep swinging once the first swing had cracked Shayna's knee.

It was Shayna's top-grossing performance to date. Through the roof. Thank god someone had captured the video, she said—she watermarked it and sold it on YouKandy.com as "Slut Gets Busted—Domme Mom Beatdown!" and made excellent passive income. Her regulars, especially the sadistic ones, were begging for more two-by-four clips. Her submissives offered miniature fortunes for a session with the domme mom. But it ended the arrangement. No more childhood bedroom, no more aunties. Shayna stayed a few nights with the store manager, Bryan, but he kept snakes in his car and the whole thing, the whole thing of Bryan, seemed off. Like how "I understand completely" is what Bryan said in response to really any word from her mouth. Clinton said she should come stay with him, absolutely rent free. She couldn't exactly believe she was doing it as she bought the plane ticket. But Clinton was awfully good-looking, and wasn't love a series of things you did in spite of how wild they were? Love is crazy, and this was crazy, so it must be love. It must.

She had no idea how hard it would be to find our place. She had to hitch a ride with a tanker truck going out to the gas pad on Bernadette's land, and her gut dropped the more they wound out into the foothills that made your ears pop, up one side and down the other, and the flat shadows of hawks slipping over the road and the last stoplight behind them by miles and miles and miles.

"Do you know that everything looks the same out here?" she asked me.

I looked outside. It was green. Although not without differences. There was a light patch on the facing hill like a bald head emerging from between breasts. Mules wandered over the breasts walking sideways in the brown grass and a tractor combed perpendicular across the temples. It was a place where the sun hit hard in the middle of the day. The clouds shifted and had a sound inside them as they moved over the sun. When they moved away again, the sun poured down more and hawks sailed all through this sound. It shone and shone. It was the blood in my head and the wind in my teeth. All the barns around had gone gray in the rain, and the boards shambled toward their peaks. I didn't always see it like that, though. When I was younger, I thought the whole world was a part of my body. I would run, I would hear the wind of my running. I thought they were the same thing. I thought if I ran hard enough, I could fall off the top of one of those ridges and go spinning away into space. I didn't really know what Shayna thought of us, any more than I could see the dark inside my head.

"I guess it does," I said. She had been pulling big clouds off her vape. It looked like a metal radio box with a kazoo in one side. I held out my hand for it. I wondered if I could draw vapor serpents like hers, which sank to the floor and disappeared, and found that I could. I really could.

The air got thin around me because I was very high up. All like that, I had become an adult. She bent my head down into the tub to rinse the dye out. My hair trailed down with the water.

"Why is he acting so weird around you?"

"I think he's just a weird guy. He doesn't know what he's doing half the time."

"I really hope he doesn't," I said. She laughed at that, but I didn't. "I don't piss my pants," I said.

"I know that."

"He told you a lie, though."

"Well," she said. "Clinton is the only man who really loves me."

"Is that true?"

She picked a shred of lip from her lip. "Oh, silly. I don't know. It's a thing people say."

XI

I had a new routine. Before dawn I walked down through the woods to Bernadette's. If Bernadette was sleeping, or upstairs at least, I first looked for her bottle. Sometimes I found an empty one on the table with an impossibly lean fume of liquid left in the bottom, and I tore the label off and put it on the porch to take with me. I went down into the cellar and looked where Virgil had. The places changed sometimes. Most often I found the bottles in the cistern, which I wondered at since it took so much work to do. Sometimes it was almost funny, where I found them. Under a shelf where splay-legged dolls sat with their faces colored blue from a marker: doll, doll, gin, doll. Sometimes I thought she'd keep track of where I had found them, but of course her memory was bad, as I would discover, and the task had a sort of matter-of-factness to it eventually.

I found it hard, though, pouring them out. I didn't like to do it. It was the worst part of the day. Unless I pried off the plastic regulator with a butter knife, which I was sometimes too inept to do, it came out slow, like it had a grudge against disappearing. The smell reminded me of gasoline. It flowered up into the air like paint. I have always loved a fume. When Virgil topped off one of the vehicles from his store of gas in the shed I sometimes would go back to where he had spilled some and hold my head over the spot where it broke up from out of the earth like another world, with its ugly edges, which I loved.

To reward myself for pouring out the gin, I would smoke a cigarette with the goats. I could try to have them like me, but instead I started to like their indifference. It's nature's genius, something that is both alive and indifferent.

It was safest if I got there before she woke up. When she was groggy she was easiest to fool. When I said good morning and called her Mom, she would just squint and say hi. She made me little bowls of oat goo, which I ate to be nice. When we talked, I could get her to wring out all the facts from a thing since her conversations went in spirals, down and down into the heart of her life.

It was not very hard to figure out. When Bernadette knew I was Cindy, she was sad because it meant her daughter was gone, or dead. When I was the slippery person, at daybreak or sundown, when I began wearing Jude's harsh black-frame glasses around the house, even though they gave me headaches and brought the world into a blurred, distant point, when I talked back to her, when I sulked, when I sang out loud, all of these things I never did at home, I believed she mistook me for her daughter, in some way. I stood in the place where Jude was supposed to be, at least. And this, I thought, was a kindness.

One day, the school bus swung down the road and came to a stop in front of Bernadette's house. I was eating mock pâté on toasts with pu-erh tea and persimmons, balancing a moldy novel in one hand, and it just seemed impossible to me, in that second, that I had ever hoisted myself up into the bus and sat for whole days talking about civics and like that.

I had not at all thought about school that whole time. As far as I was concerned, all had been forgiven—as long as I never had to go back. The squares of yellow light and the electrons that jumped from halo to halo and the gray green beans with the stringy diced ham hock (actually my favorite, even though they were gross) were funny little things from another life, and I would have them stay that way. The door cranked open. The driver hunched down to get a look at me. In one of the back windows, I could see Wyatt Tedrow from my grade wrinkling his forehead and trying to figure me out with the black hair and not at my own house. His forehead was white where it pressed against the window.

I flapped my hand in a lazy way, which I hoped would look grown, and turned the page in my book without looking up, even though I was too panicked to read. I was afraid they would drag me away. I wondered if they would talk about me, and make up stories like I had disappeared, too. I imagined my homeroom teacher calling my name into the silence.

The bus pulled away, and would not stop there again all year.

Bernadette's broken nose was healing a little wrong, but she wouldn't go to the doctor, and she couldn't remember what had happened in the first place. Sometimes I caught her pressing it in places and wincing, and I would ask how her face felt.

"You know, it usually feels just fine, but today for some reason. I don't know. Achy? I feel like I should have an aspirin. Or a drink." She returned to this last point often. There was a glare in the sky, so she should probably put on a hat, or get a drink. She had read about a beautiful love story between a waitress and a cop, and could I sit down and listen for a minute to how wonderful it was, and get her a drink. It was the day of Saint Trea, and we should celebrate by eating oranges. And orange is lovely in hot toddies, so why don't I bring out the bottle. I didn't say no. I had stopped pouring out the bottles. They were my best disguise, after all.

Virgil had made it clear my real job was to keep Bernadette from killing herself by accident, which she could easily do falling down the stairs, burning the house down, or breathing her sick back down into her lungs. The pilot light was busted on her stove so you had to kiss on it with a lit match, but she'd be in the middle of telling me about the Hapsburg Empire and forget, with the gas hissing out god knows how long. ("They say Leopold's jaw was so deformed that his mouth filled with water when it rained.") In between seeing to that, I cleaned things. I took everything down from the high places and wiped it off with a wet rag, all her carved totems and semiprecious stones and feathers and pieces of sentimental tin. She didn't like that I touched these things and claimed in fact that they had a particular order and formed triads and hexagons and trines I could know nothing about, but unless she saw me messing with them explicitly she didn't seem to notice.

She was easy to manipulate. I wish it had not been so. But either from grief or from drinking she couldn't keep a thought in her head for longer than five minutes most of the time, longer than any time I was in the room with her. When I left, or she left, the scene was reset. There was nothing I could do to keep from having the same conversations with her eighty times a day. Like:

"Where's my black beaded sweater?"

"It's too hot for a sweater."

"Oh, I know that. But I want to know where it is."

"Why."

"I want to be sure you didn't take it."

"I don't want your dirty old sweater," I said. "I don't care." Too harsh. Leave the room, begin again.

"Honey, have you seen my black beaded sweater?"

"Sorry, I haven't."

"You took it."

"Ma. It's right here." The sweater was spread in a cross on the back of the couch. She was sitting on it, in fact. It floated up behind her like an evil shadow.

"Oh," she said. She craned around and petted it, reassured of its presence. "Good. It's my favorite one. I got it in Redondo Beach, you know."

"What's Redondo Beach?"

"It's a place in California where they sell you the very soul of a fish on a platter for one thin dime."

"What's California like?"

"Serene. Yet dark. It's a frightening place, but the flowers are beautiful." It was getting dark. The air went out of the room with a hiss. Lamplight moved on the beading and it looked like a crawling thing. Bernadette went to put on the kettle. She had already put it on and forgotten about it twice that evening. I could tell the handle was still hot because she jumped her hand back away from it, though she said nothing. She dipped the match into the burner and the flame boomed up. I had thrown away the other spent matches. She always thought it was for the first time, everything.

She went back to the couch and took up her crossword puzzle again. And asked me what's this and what's that, the Tiber, the emu, pahoehoe, Tiger Woods.

"Where's my black beaded sweater?"

"It's too hot for a sweater."

"Oh, I know that. I just want to know where it is."

"Why."

"I want to be sure you didn't take it."

"I don't want your nasty old sweater. Besides, I don't wear black. It's unbecoming of a young girl." This is just the kind of airy thing I, Cindy, would have never said.

"You took it!"

"Ma. Behind you."

"Oh. Well, good. You know, it's my favorite one."

"Redondo Beach," I said.

"Redondo Beach! I used to sing there, if you didn't know."

"Not to the beach! You would sound crazy. They would have arrested you."

"Hah. They would like to have, believe me. No, in a bar. It was the most beautiful bar. The air inside felt ancient. The wine was free, but you had to pay for the use of the glass. I've forgotten why. Some kind of law, I guess."

When her tea was ready, I'd bring it in and sit with her a minute. We'd look over the crossword. And Virgil came at dark, to cozy me up and take me back up the hill to home with the incense still flowing from my clothes, from the places where my pulse heated up. I figured she couldn't get into much trouble if I was paying attention to how much she drank. She put it in her tea. She was generally starting to get sloshy by the time Virgil showed up, so I hid everything in spots of my own devising. Every night, I told Bernadette I was going to a sleepover at Kayla's. Sometimes she seemed sad when I told her. Other days she waved me off without looking up from her book.

I think that even as many times as she asked me who I was, what I was doing in her house, there were hundreds more times she wondered and didn't say it. She still had enough wit to sustain some pride. It embarrassed her not to know. She was aware that she ought to know what I was doing there with the wrench scuttling around under the counter to turn the gas back on. She had probably tried to make a cup of tea in the middle of the night and wondered why this act would not be allowed. So much worse than this, she would be alone in it. I probably didn't look like an intruder in my sock feet and with Mondo leaning against my shins while I turned the pages of an old Met catalog. I could tell she was covering when she fluffed up her hair at the nape of her neck, a thing girls do. A thing I did, which she might have even copied from me to earn some unconscious favor.

And in those moments, too, it was only safe to speak of the things that were around us and equally visible to us and not related especially to any sense of history. We could not talk, for example, about whatever we had done yesterday. It would only become clear that she did not remember. We could not talk either about me. Possibly I had already told her everything about my life. I might have emerged just before the moments that tied themselves together had broken all apart on her, and it would be hurtful to remind me of this, of how little I could mean to her.

So instead, Bernadette would choose something in the room and comment on it, as if it were the first time she had noticed it in all these years. But the trouble was instead, then, that she chose the same few things to comment on. One was a set of green dominoes laid out in some almost totemic pattern, one was a sun-stained packet of aster seeds folded in half to accommodate the wobbling table. One was the picture of Sister Rosetta Tharpe taped to the refrigerator, and did I know that Bernadette had met her once? Why, yes, I did. But I had to pretend otherwise.

We talked about the goats every day. They were our soap opera, our royal family, our tabloids and actresses gone to fat. Bernadette pointed out the way Dolores's hind legs were mussed over with spume, dirt. It was a sign she had just been mounted. The billy pissed on himself to get smelly enough for mating and left his dirt on the girls. The next day, it was Panda Jane with the dirty hind parts. I pretended to be scandalized, but only because Bernadette loved so much to tease me. Really, I thought this was unremarkable. But I loved how it made Bernadette laugh.

One of the does was clumsy. She could be counted on to knock over a pail of water, even a full one. She was so friendly she stepped on my feet. What was her name, I wanted to know.

"Ann Richards," Bernadette said. "She's got a drinking problem, but you know, she's just *so brave*." And she laughed and laughed. Well, I didn't know who Ann Richards was. But I laughed, too, because it was a thing for us to do together.

At home, I found it helped me, this habit of dwelling only in the things I could see. I could crawl from one moment to the blank vista of the next. When Clinton hugged me too long and felt the bra strap through my T-shirt, I could go blank into the dark parts of the plain air, the parts that are always there and which you can travel into. Moment, moment, moment. I shaved off one moment and left it behind. I was becoming someone he couldn't keep track of, and he had no idea. At home, we were always watching a courtroom TV show about roommates who couldn't agree whose turn it was to pay for cable. At Bernadette's, I ate pomegranates and read Khalil Gibran. I kept waiting for someone to enforce a normal bedtime, or at least ask where did I get the small black cherry candle I was now burning in my room to read by, what was the matter with my face, because my face was looking different. Even apart from the makeup and hair dye, I knew something new was starting to show up there.

XII

Why was it, I can't remember now. I think I had fallen down in the goat berries and gotten them all over my shirt, or possibly I was just dusty from moving around in the barn. But anyway I needed a change of clothes, and everything in the hampers had been there who knows how long, and reeked like mink marks, so I decided to wear something of Jude's.

I knew it was wrong to go into Jude's room. There was still some investigation tape across the door. I had to duck under to get inside. I couldn't believe how many things Jude had. A shoebox of nail polish bottles had been dumped out on the rag rug, eighty kinds. They were all across the floor, and left here and there where detectives had been through them.

Most of her clothes were on the floor of the closet, things cramped together with trash, and I saw a blister packet of birth control pills, which made me ache for her privacy, even while I trampled it. I wanted to leave her alone, but I wanted, too, to bury myself in the stuff that smelled like her, some harsh perfume like burning wood. It didn't seem like it would be so wrong to take one of the dresses off the hanger. I was covered in goat berries, after all. I had to wear something clean. The dress was a black slippery thing with a drawstring waist and no sleeves and even right against my skin it felt like an animal. My blood warmed it up right away.

Maybe it was because the dress felt good. It felt good in a way my own clothes never did. Like I had skinned a lake and was wearing its hide on me. I'm saying this, I'm trying to explain. I saw the little vial of neroli oil, plain, with a white cap and a sticker almost rubbed off. I put it around my jaw and on my wrists like I had heard about. I felt like I should sit with my skirt circling me in the grass and toss an apple into the sun. I was not myself. My lungs were bigger. The sun was shaping a cloud and letting the light get choked up behind it. Swift, like it happens here often, the panels of light just dropping away in an instant. I had no use for Cindy anymore. So I put on more of the missing girl's things. Her bracelets. She had stacks of them, the aluminum ones with diamond shapes cut in the metal. And because I liked the way they slid over my arms I also was touching at my hair and I twisted it up with a barrette. I don't have any more words for it now. My spine was long. I felt like I had grown a tail, a halo, a claw.

My experimental walk down the hallway to the bathroom, all the time I was nervous to see myself. But Cindy wasn't there. With Jude's clothes on me, my new muscles slipping up under my skin, she wasn't there. This was a boat to go over a green ocean in, and there could be bells ringing somewhere. Hello, Marilou! I saw the word *ITALY* lit up in capitals, or I thought I did. The fish in my stomach coursed together by drumbeat or scattered. *Help!* I thought. I think I even laughed.

I must have looked at myself a long time like that.

Bernadette came into the bathroom. For some reason, this felt much more serious than my previous attempts at dissolving myself into Jude. Maybe I had begun to fool myself in some much more essential way. And possibly I'd already laid in all of the damage much earlier, in some instant that still eludes me. But I do know: This is where I would stop it, if I could actually go back and do such a thing. My heart hammered some warnings to me. I saw her tumbled hair behind me in the mirror. I hadn't thought it through, of course. I had not thought what to say to her, standing there in her daughter's dress, and with her jewelry warming up by my wrists. And with her neroli-oil perfume heated by my skin running out into the world.

I thought she might spank me again. Or haul me up and throw me out. But she passed lightly behind me and stepped over to the commode. She hiked up her skirt and peed, her face blank as an animal's. Then she paced again behind me, wetted her hands in the faucet, and patted herself with the water under her armpits. She smiled at me, licked a finger, and pushed away a sleep crumb from my cheek. When Virgil came to pick me up that night, I cried a little, going away, watching Mondo run out into the road behind us.

For fun, we started calling the tip line on the flyer Alistair Vanderjohn had left at Pecjak's. Shayna knew someone who did it full time in Texas. He would look up all the things on the Crime Stoppers website and call a bunch of times to say he saw speeding cars of various descriptions leaving the scene of the shooting or robbery or whatever. Sometimes he gave Shayna a cut for calling in the tips because the regular Crime Stoppers operators were getting to know the sound of his voice, even when he made it high or spoke through a sock. Shayna knew the whole deal. He ran an algorithm to determine the most common alphanumeric combos on plates. He listened to the scanner radio constantly. He ran it all night while he was sleeping. And sometimes, when he went around he found a place that just had a bad feeling in it. It might just be a strip mall doughnut shop or a roadside beauty school, anyplace with a bad sparkle in the air. It didn't matter. He called it in. Sometimes he just made shit up. He made up women who did bad things and told the tip line about their heart-shaped mouths and chestnut ringlets and where the moles were on their faces and where they dumped the bodies. Crazy enough, those were just slightly more likely to pay out. "It's a little like being a psychic," Shayna said. "He helped catch a mom who left her babies chained up in a storage locker, just because he had a feeling. He called in and said it was a redheaded woman who drove a purple PT Cruiser. Broke the case wide open. He made ten grand on that one alone."

So Shayna called and called about Jude:

"I saw her get in a red car."

"I saw her get in a blue car."

"She got on a 250cc motorcycle of some kind."

"She became a Scientologist and signed up to do the thing? Where you live on a ship?"

"I saw her just ten minutes ago at the Wendy's off I-79. She was with an obese man in mesh shorts."

"She was wearing a headscarf."

"They cut off all her hair."

"She's in a barn somewhere near the Mason-Dixon Line."

"She was sold to a tech billionaire. No, I don't know what for."

"She jumped off the bridge, the big one over the gorge. The, I don't know, the gorge bridge? No, I'm not laughing."

She made a separate call for each. Each time, she wrote down a seven-digit number on the back of the flyer.

"OK, the guy's catching on to me. Your turn."

"I don't know what to say."

"Baby, just close your eyes and see something. Then tell him what you saw." She handed me the pen and the flyer. "Just don't make it too specific or it won't work."

I dialed the number. "She ran away to the ocean," I said. "She's sitting on a rock right now."

"Excuse me?"

"Jude. That's where she is."

"Who?"

"Jude. Vanderjohn? She's missing?"

"She's on a rock—by the ocean?"

"That's what I saw when I closed my eyes."

"This is not a prank, young lady."

"OK, sorry," I said. He didn't give me a claim number.

I was across the way with Bernadette's goats when a little sky-blue sedan pulled up and stopped my heart. Nobody was supposed to come by that I knew of, and I had never seen the car before. People's cars always looked to me like an extension of their face. Melda McConaughey's rusted-out bug looked like Shelley Duvall, for example. But the man I had seen at Pecjak's—Jude's father—got out and pulled a banker's box from the trunk and went right on in the door like he had been expected. I was terribly afraid he would turn and see me watching him. Just like that, he looked up and waved hello.

The truth is, I had been ducking Bernadette's friends ever since I had decided to dye my hair black and become the slippery person. It would become too complicated to keep up my trick if anyone was there to ask questions, and I'm sad to say it, but lots of people are quick to take an out, and not have to drive halfway across the county to sit in a dim living room and drink bitter tea and get dog hair all over themselves. So I told Bernadette's friends, when they called, that she was feeling unwell and I was just down the road to bring her a casserole but they shouldn't bother. I didn't have to tell anyone twice. It didn't really occur to me that anyone would drop in without calling. Or had I left the phone unattended? I considered unplugging the cord whenever I watered the goats or left for the day, or even keeping it in my pocket so as to avoid any more surprises.

They weren't in the front room, so I snuck around the back of the house and hovered myself down on my heels below the kitchen window. I could hear papers slithering across the table, and my own ragged heartbeat, which I tried to stiffen.

"Bernie. Bernie. It's not going to help. You've got to look at it the way it is." His voice sounded a little tired, but not angry.

"It's just so good to see you, Alistair. Let's put it all behind us. Let's go back to Chico. I've had enough of this place. Oh, I'm sick to death of it. I want to see the sky again."

"Here's the main thing, OK? We've got to keep her face out there. I've been talking to the detectives, and they say that's the way to go."

"Whose face, baby?"

"Jude. Jude is missing."

"I swear to god, Alistair. You can't come down here and chew on my ass every time she complains about something I've done."

"I assure you, I didn't come to chew your ass. Our girl is missing."

"Jude and Virgil are off on a wild teenage love trip. You're just a smother. And I will not subject my baby to these fear-based beliefs of yours. Besides, she's just across the road with the goats. Or her friend is. Well, I don't know what they're doing. You go look for yourself."

"I saw her—that's Virgil's sister, isn't it?"

"Well, I don't keep track of Jude's friends. But yes."

"She's by herself. Jude is missing. Jude isn't here."

"Why do you keep saying that? We just painted our nails this morning. We're going to make banana bread."

"Bernadette. I'm not going to do it. I'm not going round and round with you, especially not if you've been drinking." As far as I knew, she hadn't been, but I could see how he'd be confused. Her memory was shot so it didn't much matter, actually. A big silence spilled out and out like oil on water, and then I heard her chair creak.

"You know, I'm kind of tired," she said. "You should probably go. I am just too weary for all this. If you want to nail me to the cross, you'll just have to come back tomorrow."

“I’m leaving tonight. Driving right to the airport.”

“Airport! Well, take me with you, then. Take me back to Chico, darling. I’ve had enough of this place. I miss seeing the sky. Oh, I am heavy sick of not seeing the sky.”

I braced for whatever Mr. Vanderjohn was about to say to that, but then on the other side of that silence, I heard him crying. It was shuddery. It sounded like he was chipping pieces off a big rock, but trying to be quiet about it. I didn’t know what to do. It seemed silly to keep hiding since he had recognized me, but neither did I want to see a crying man. It seemed like if I looked, he would know something about me which I hid desperately. He cried for what seemed a long time. My legs were burning and my heels had gone numb, but I couldn’t move.

Finally I heard the screen door, and then the car starting up. He hadn’t said good-bye. Probably he knew there was no reason in it. I gave it a few more minutes before I came inside. I was hoping Bernadette would be untroubled by recent memory so I could ply her toward some safe activity instead, but she was holding one of the flyers right up under her nose.

“Who are you?” She sounded puzzled, and not angry, but I didn’t want to risk the mood going bad.

I found a fresh bottle of gin and poured it half with Coca-Cola into her travel mug and took it to where she sat.

“I’ll trade you,” I said, and shoved the mug into her hand. The stack of flyers I took upstairs with me to destroy.

XIII

This one I heard from Sissy Pecjak, whose brother was a hospital orderly. Apparently, when they didn't find any hint of Jude in the correctional system, the police began checking the hospitals. In Mon General, they found a girl who couldn't remember her name. She matched Jude's description. She had not produced any ID. The hospital records averred someone had left her in one of the courtesy wheelchairs at the emergency entrance on May 19, a few days after Jude's last sighting. She had been signed in under the name Janet Lockjaw, which afterward it was clear had been some species of joke.

Apart from being severely malnourished, she carried a bone infection in her jaw. She couldn't or wouldn't say where she had been. But when they asked if her name was Judith Vanderjohn, she said yes. When they asked her if she lived in Deep Valley with her mother, she said yes. Was she hurt? Yes. Who did this to her? Yes. Then she switched to saying Wow. She stayed stuck on Wow. Wow, wow, wow. Wowowowowow. The nurses, when they thought nobody was listening, called her the Human Ambulance.

In a different hospital, they found another black girl who said she wasn't who she said she was. She had also been dumped in a courtesy wheelchair, although all she needed was a dose of Narcan. They had kept her on psych eval for a week because she had self-administered cuts on her arms and claimed no knowledge of the United States of America.

Instead she insisted she had come from another world. You think this place is real, but it's not, she said. This is a display, like fireworks. Very pretty. But not real. She nevertheless proceeded to give the police a full description, address, and Social Security number for her ex-boyfriend, and advised them as to which drawers in his mother's china hutch hid his kiddie porn hard drives. Detective Torboli made the arrests. Her information closed down a handful of small-timers. When he went back to tell her the outcome, she had discharged herself and disappeared. He found her months later living in one of the halfway houses. She was running a fierce shadow business doing manicures for the other girls. She had made a detailing paintbrush out of her own hair taped with exquisite precision to a golf pencil, and she accepted cigarettes, Red Bull, or dish chores in payment for her art. All the fractional housing girls lit their smokes and picked their eyebrows with landscaped fingernails of painted tigers and pink lightning. She thanked Detective Torboli for what he had done, although she maintained that everything was a dharma, and all dharmas should be regarded as dreams.

I did not say what I was or wasn't. This was a parlor game. Like the day we played charades: Bernadette made the slips of pink paper for the punch bowl, and they said things like JUNKIE, FARMER, SCIENTIST, KING KONG. CHER. She got drunk. A little too early in the afternoon, but the day was warm and I could not really argue with gin and ice and gin. It was my time and I felt fat. A rose is. The dew of a frigid October. Buster Keaton's beautiful eyes. I said there was no way to act this one out. HERACLITUS? Who the hell? She tried to charade it by putting her arched pale foot again and again down on the red-and-blue carpet. I did not of course then know the old thing about the twice-stepped-in river. Mine were too simple: SUNSHINE, SHOTGUN, FRYPAN. No challenge, said Bernadette, although I maintain sunshine is difficult to act out. How? Do you point to the sky, to your arm, your heart? I pulled another pink card. It said OCEAN. According to the impossible rules I had to show the broken strip of film from my childhood and hope it telegraphed something guessable. Which was all: hay dazzle, green fire, a black bird guzzling up the gasoline where it spilled. Most mandatory days on holidays, having fun with the whole family. Spending time together, the muscles clank. You pay out the chain into a depthless lake, but the bottom is so soft you miss the glitch when the anchor hits. I said who is Buster Keaton anyway. Bernadette said he was very athletic. But neurotic.

She liked to trick the gas men, when one of them needed to come down to the house to check some surveyor's mark or when they stood there in the edge of the maples to smoke. Come on down here, she'd say. Have you some lemonade. This is my girlfriend Ann Richards—and she'd push me into their work-burned hands. Oh yes, me and Ann Richards, we are having a beautiful Sunday. Monday? Have it your way, I'm not bothered. They bore it decent. One of them would stand around talking about happy nonsense with his gloves shoved down in his back pockets, pinging his eyes between the two of us like he could almost smell the trick. The foreman sometimes left a box of doughnuts.

Once, I told Bernadette it was my birthday, just to see what she would do.

"My god, is it January already? Of course. Of course. Goodness. We'll have to tell your fortune immediately. There's no better day, really. The birthdays are how you can really know." She put her thumb over the sun and frowned. "I wish you'd said something a bit earlier, Ann Richards. We're losing the light already. We'll have to hurry to do this right."

She sat me at the table and brought out a photocopied piece of paper with a circle and pentagram inside it. She bid me close my eyes and then snatched a clot of hair from the top of my head and put it in the middle. It looked like a strange filmy root. I was afraid to breathe too hard and set it scouring off the table, except of course it had come from my own head and more could be gotten. In her left hand, she held the pendulum with the clear column of quartz at the end, the string trained around her index finger. With her right hand, she pressed down upon my shoulder and felt around on my face.

"OK, I've got it. What do you want to know about yourself?"

"What will I be?"

"Be? Be? Nope. Too tricky. Start with something little."

"What will happen to me tomorrow?" The pendulum took up a little orbit. Bernadette placed her finger here and there on the chart. At one point, it swung back around the other way.

"Tomorrow you will cross a river. From the other side, you will see the truth."

"Will I ever fall in love?"

"Yes, one time. But it will be all you need."

"Am I good?"

"Sweetie," she said. "Of course."

"What will I be?"

She took a long time. She touched my chin and nose and wagged her fingers back and forth over my forehead. Her face soured, and she checked those places again. The pendulum danced all over. She shook out her hand and resumed. It really was my birthday. I hadn't told anyone, but I was sure that it would make what she said especially true.

"What is it? What is it saying?"

"You will be a moth."

"What does that mean?"

"Well, I don't know! I only know the answers. I don't ever know why they are right."

XIV

Dark came on earlier. The blue light had a glassy depth to it. Bernadette said it was the hours before the moon rose that made the color reverberate in its vaulted bowl over us. The first stars were scrawled in, and Virgil was late getting me. When I called at the house nobody answered. I had already shut down the house for the night, but Bernadette kept me company on the porch wrapped in a blanket. She had a little cigar. It looked like she was smoking a child's finger. I wasn't wrapped in a blanket because I was certain Virgil would be there any second.

But the night got deeper and instead the lights over the barn eaves up and down the road began casting down orange in the dark with the moths churning up in them. I didn't want to go inside because that would mean something had gone wrong with Virgil and I was admitting that it was a little scary. He had never not come to get me. He had never even been late. I walked out to the road, to see if I could spot his headlights.

And I had never been in Bernadette's house through the night before. I usually left when the light was still bending down hard upon everything. I walked a little ways up the gravel toward the road like that would make me hear the truck coming. I had my grocery sack with my things in it—a set of coins we'd found behind the bookcase, and a bag of orange peels I was drying out on the radiators as a project. But the night made its one sound, *shiny shiny*, and the silence jingled with nothing to sop it up or get in its way.

When I turned back to the house, I felt like I saw it for the first time. It was a lantern on the slope and inside the crud of fingerprints and handprints just looked soft yellow everywhere. It was something else. Beautiful. As I had never truly seen it before, I felt somewhat shy now to walk back up to it. But I sat at Bernadette's feet. I had told her that I was supposed to have a sleepover at a friend's house, and the friend's mom was just late. She suggested that maybe I should call my friend. I didn't feel like reminding her that I had already called twice. I had listened to it ring through.

"You seem worried," she said.

"Nothing," I said. "There's nothing for me to worry about."

"That's not how it feels." She put her hand on my back. I tried hard not to tense it up. "I can feel it right here."

"I'm fine!"

"I really do wish you'd tell me, honey. I can tell. It's been hard for a while. You've been different." The first two tears fell straight from my eyes because I was looking down. The shame of it, to cry for being given a mistaken kindness, made me lose my iron. I pressed my jaw down hard against my chest.

Shayna didn't find Jude's disappearance mysterious. She said the girl got pregnant and split for terror or died bleeding on the linoleum of a doctor's home kitchen, or she was sick in the head for all-time reasons that will be known as classics forever: Teenage! Teenage! Teenage! And what else is there? I knew it. I wrote the things to myself on my legs high up where my shorts covered. *L-O-V-E* I wrote with a safety pin, just lightly so it was a pale scrape. I never could draw my own blood. Even teenage, I wasn't that kind.

But also what I thought about it was: We were the same as animals anyway. And an animal leaves its home for its own compelling reasons.

Didn't I? The logic runs on a track small as a toy train, just around and around. I can neither confirm nor deny. But I guess this is what makes me true rural.

I would have been Jude a million times if you had asked me every day of the million. Gravity did not knit her so hard to this earth, I thought. Even disappeared and tortured, I wanted to be her and not myself. Jude, it seemed to me, had projected her personal world into the world so hard that it pulled her inside out. I had to love that kind of trouble from a distance because I couldn't make it mine. Now, that's a sick thing to say. But it was true that I envied something I so totally misunderstood.

Bernadette rubbed her hands against each other and laid them on my back. I felt like I was being prepared for a mythic journey. I would get to go somewhere dangerous alone trusted as an envoy, maybe that was the feeling. Though I was light I was not often lifted up, any part. She took the shawl off her own shoulders and laid it on mine. It got colder.

That was the night they arrested Virgil, although I wouldn't know about it until later. A car wash attendant found a wallet and cell phone wedged under the trunk mat in Amber's car when she had it detailed. Both were Jude's. It made sense—the girls had been in a hurry to get away from the campsite and thrown their things into the cars to sort out later. She brought it right to the police, wrapped up in a Giant Eagle bag. Just like that, the theory of Jude the runaway was dead. Suddenly, it seemed wrong to them how much talking Virgil had been able to do on his conviction that Jude had run away. Just the week before, he told the detectives how Bernadette beat her daughter. He had seen it under Jude's clothes. Still he loved Bernadette. She was almost more a mother than his own mother, even if she had some harsh ways. The police had been about set to stop looking for Jude entirely, not that they ever had much to go on. So when Amber found Jude's things, the case shaped up all of a sudden.

And it was more than this: Virgil had apparently stolen Bernadette's Tiffany silver at some point over the summer, and tried to sell it to the very same antiques dealer who had appraised it for Bernadette the year before. The dealer recognized an irregularity in the dessert forks. When they pressed Virgil about the silver, they caught him in some other lies. I don't know what about, but it looked pretty bad for him.

I didn't know any of this then. Instead, I was feeling very sorry for myself, forgotten and feeling it in the pit of my stomach, which was suddenly as empty as a bell. What would I do if Virgil never came? I sat there trying to figure how I would make my way through the dim woods. I should be no fool about darkness since I grew up in that place, but it had always a waiting kind of silence to it and I never much liked going away from the house when night was soaking through the trees. Bernadette was shivering. So was I. Actually, I was furious. Where were they, any of my family? Bernadette's house was feeling more like home, and it's true that I loved it, but some part of me was also waiting for them to say enough and drag me back. Who would let me do such a thing? They didn't care, and here was the proof. In my mind, I snipped the threads between us. I wouldn't concern myself with them any more than they concerned themselves with me. So I let Bernadette bring me inside. Her hand on the back of my shoulders, it was somehow clearing out the space before me for me to move through it. Easier than usual. We went up the stairs, past the bathroom and the boxes of junk in the hallway and the night with no curtains was shuddering in at us with the drafts, the huge dark air wandering through my ribs. It didn't make a difference. It was a spell. I'd ruin it to speak and so I didn't.

Jude's room still had the police tape blocking it. I had ducked under it every time I'd snuck in to steal her clothes. Bernadette pulled up the tape at one edge and it fluttered down, so we were in. The room smelled sort of wet. A window was open. I watched her pull the bedding up. Jammed under the pillow there was a paperback painted green on the page edges. I sat in the shallow divot and then gave over everything,

everything. I mean that I lay down. Like you would lie down next to a river and die. Bernadette closed the bed over me and who were we in that moment. I beg of you, I beg of you. You tell me. You tell me. She plugged in a night light shaped like a seashell. I closed my eyes and saw the usual thing, the red and blue temples, before I went to sleep.

XV

The year I went back to school, I had a therapist for a little while. She was free, or she was free for me, anyway. A *People* magazine story had made me famous, temporarily, but not in a way I liked or could manage. I didn't know how to go back to living with my mother as if the rest of these things hadn't happened. I knew I wasn't doing a convincing job of being a person, just from the way that the teachers looked at me, but I didn't know what I was doing wrong. The guidance counselor drove me to the therapist herself, and dropped me back at the school afterward to ride the activity bus home. She sent me home with papers that made it seem like I was in detention. I didn't realize until later she was covering in case my mom wouldn't let me go to therapy. Which just shows how little she understood my situation—I had been signing my own report cards and permission slips for years. She seemed to enjoy feeling like she was doing an outlaw thing in helping me. She had this very tense, serious way of asking if I wanted to pick the radio station. If I played along (shyly brave, terse/poetic), she'd get us cheeseburgers on the way back.

I liked going to the therapist. I got the sense from the building that other people were paying a lot of money to sit there and look at the black-and-white photographs she had hung in the beige chill of her office.

It was a strange building. The outside was tiled up to the roof in green, something that looked like it had been chipped off of a seashell. Every other building on the block was an old-age home. Every building, including Dr. Holden's office, had a parking loop in front like a hotel, and somebody was always waiting desolate there to be picked up. They wore loose pastel clothes but you could still see the bodies underneath them had been squashed in evil ways to look old and flesh bubbled out wrongly under armpits and over guts. I loved it, walking in there. No matter what else I could feel the essential column of my body under me, the muscle in it, the rightness of the gristle and bone which stood me up straight on one end and pushed me around the skin of the earth in a more or less decent way.

For some reason, the walls and ceiling were covered with the same brown carpet they used on the floor. Dr. Holden had long gray hair, very pretty. She wore large necklaces with chocks of amber suspended by rope and wire, earrings like little yellow eyes dangling from under her hair. She wrote on a yellow legal pad while I talked. Sometimes she didn't write anything, but watched me. She reminded me of someone I liked, and I couldn't figure it out for such a long time. It didn't matter what I said. Her face never moved.

I told her about all the lipsticks I stole throughout my life, Shayna, the way I used to flash the cars that drove by. It felt like I told Dr. Holden the same things every session, but we both knew there was something I refused to say. Every time she asked me to turn out my pockets, I had the same inventory, the same magical traveling penny that showed up there and lay under all of my thoughts, and no matter how different and particular I felt myself to be, it seemed I had only really one fact about myself, which was what I had done to Jude. And I wouldn't say it. I know it isn't supposed to work this way, therapy, but I found it depressing that there was nothing else to my life but its own straw and dust and stuffing.

Sometimes she let me talk about things that didn't go anywhere. I told her how I had always seen an emptiness in everything, calm and almost friendly. It rang and rang like a white room. And sometimes it made things sparkle in unreliable ways, and how people smiled in the grocery store seemed suddenly troubling. Sometimes she asked me about Virgil, but with Virgil I only talked about how smart he was at whistling, his made-up preacher voice.

I thought I would shock Dr. Holden by saying how much I loved living with Bernadette. I loved watching Jude's skirts luft down around my legs as I sat under a crabapple to read the dirty yellow copy of *Miss Lonelyhearts* I had found by the bathtub, letting my hand dream through my hair precisely, so exactly unlike Cindy in the doing. I loved the stains the tumbled crabapples left on my skirt—or I loved not caring about them because I was so beautiful that they didn't matter or in fact made me more so for not caring. I could fill my mouth with grapes to almost choke me, and be laughing with the sun in my hair. I loved being hungry because I could eat cheese and guava sandwiches until their lust was gone. The lust moved to other things, even water. Even plain, cold water. I loved the empty pillow in my head listening to Bernadette's jazz records, I loved that my little tits were just a handful of porridge. I loved how Panda Jane followed me through the fields. I loved the grain of my sweat sparkling in my hair after we had been hauling the wood or bent into the earth pulling chickweed. I loved finding what I loved. I found it by echo. *Mine, mine, mine*, I would think. *This world is mine. It is mine. It is mine.*

It didn't matter how many times I told her about it. She stared up sometimes from her notes. She never seemed shocked. She looked at me like my face was a long hallway, and I was somewhere at the back, playing with my fingers, wiping up dust with my fingers. She wasn't wrong. I was back there, all the way. I would walk back out past the old people in their gowns, attended by IV trolleys, while the squat buses kneeled to take them off in every direction, and I tried to think about who Dr. Holden reminded me of.

It was the goats, of course. They had looked at me the same way when I snuck outside with a stolen cigarette after I had spent the gin down the sink, and even after I had started keeping a little jam jar of it in reserve for myself, which I drank warm, hot, really, in the smallest sips like it could go and sew my face up for all time, and I might never have to talk to anyone again.

I knew Dr. Holden was a great therapist because she didn't believe anything I said.

Bernadette seemed to get better. The weather stopped shifting. The hot gorges of air stopped turning and shimmering over the garden. No more bright days flowering up in the middle of the week, and the weather began to sustain a long slide into winter. I think it was easier for her then, to know what would more or less happen a few days in a row. I didn't go home anymore. She wore her black beaded sweater all through the morning and only took it off in the afternoon when the air would seem to heat and pile up around us, moving so little in the shade that it would boil us, but as soon as the sun dropped behind the hills it went crisp right away, like somebody had turned a switch.

Our days fell into a kind of ordinary beauty. Mondo nipped the goats back into their bitten-down circle when they tried to slip up into the patch of saplings. I made coffee. I fixed toast lined with the orange stewed mussels Bernadette liked and which I could never get a taste for. They felt like boiled erasers, earlobes, something that should still be attached to a body somewhere. I took the plate outside and watched her eat while the dew faded up from the grass and it went dark in the sun. I stopped hiding the gin bottles entirely. I really thought if I kept an eye on her drinking I could make it work out. There seemed to be a spot between the first drink and falling down where she loved me.

This is funny. I didn't know what soy sauce was when I moved into Bernadette's. She liked to make a dish with green beans and ground beef and ginger. When we ate it, which was almost once a week, she put a little bottle of ink on the table. The bottle was not marked. She dumped jots of it on her plate. She was always doing things I couldn't understand. Keeping up with her laws was impossible, and neither was it workable to follow her lead. Once, I tried to help her fold an afghan which she was beating against the side of the sofa, and she shooed me away, saying, "No, no virgins may assist me."

I found out later that she decanted the stuff from a rectangular can kept in the basement. It looked exactly like a gas can except its label was something like River Pearl or Black River or Black Swan, and there was a swan with its head knocked in reverie. But it looked just like ink to me. The bottle was squat, exactly like I imagined an ink bottle might look.

So much of her custom was strange to me. We ate dinner by candlelight, when the electric worked perfectly fine and the bill was all paid. Some of her things were not to go in the washing machine. She shrieked when she found me tossing a black blouse with white chrysanthemums in with the bedsheets. The dirt on carrots was fine to eat. To wash them off first was prissy. But the lettuces swam in a tin bowl of ice water until all their grit had sifted out. We sat in front of the wood stove with a picture book from a museum, and she wanted me to say what was happening in each picture. I thought she wanted me to sound intelligent, and I tried to. But what made her really happy was when I got sick of that and said instead exactly what I thought, which is that the saints looked like droolers and Mary looked kind of full of herself.

I devised a method: Whatever I thought, I did the opposite. I cried at beautiful moments. I ate the hated persimmons, even the gluey ones. I told her I would rather die than look average.

But sousing my food with ink was too much. I watched it each week. She moved it from the cupboard when she set the table. She returned it after the meal. It was not consulted the rest of the time. It had no special roles. It could have been a lucky totem. She had lots of these. Bernadette put a laminar clay elephant in the tub with her when she bathed, then dried it with the corner of her towel and propped it back in the window. Sometimes, she would stand abruptly, jot something down on a yellow legal pad, then go outside and lay the page flat on the grass, drop a burning match onto it, and watch it warp away. It was a minor mystery. If it made her happy, I was happy to let her keep casting her intentions around us with totems and indexes.

Eventually, I did it. I dropped dark slashes of the stuff all over my plate. Bernadette had been picking at me over dinner. Why did I insist on shaving my armpits? It was so pleading. Why did I look at her like a guppy? I was too eager. Why did I put pickle juice in the potato salad? Well, I thought everyone did that. I was pissed at her, and so I thought: *Here you go, you big-panties bitch. I'm going to eat all your uppity spiritual ink and just to hell with you.* The salt burned because I put on too much—how was I supposed to know its evil potency? It pulled all the spit down to my gums. But I ate it all, and smiled, and learned my life.

And then three things happened. The weather broke hard and everything was washed silver in the mornings. The light was gone down to nothing almost right away. It felt like midnight by the time I was done making dinner.

Deer season began, and the days had more gun blasts in them quite suddenly. Each one sounded like a big round hole of cannon fire in the sky, something with ragged, fizzy edges. I thought of a darkness opening up right in the air where the bullet ripped through to go heart, heart, heart toward its heat.

And at night, what the hunters would do is look for where the deer liked to go. They tracked them with flashlights, just big utility ones which they shined through the windows of a truck cab. The lights chased over fields like a devil thing. Like any light, they could move so fast from near to far it was like a magic creature from a storybook. I could see them from Bernadette's sitting room scanning the goats' field across the road. Sometimes they caught sight of a deer and it froze from its panic, or sometimes also they caught a goat. They always looked to me unreal when they were trapped like that, with their edges turned to flame and all the little dust sparkles drifting down around them. Which were always there, but it required a flashlight to see that the world was really shot through with such a glamorous dust.

We didn't get spotters up on the ridge because it was too hard to drive the bent spine of road and follow the spotlight's roaming blot into anywhere. It would go jagged and crash upward or downward crazily and no point in it. In the bottoms, where the valley platted out in a floodplain around the crick, it was easier to sight things.

So I guess I never had the experience of being seen when the spotters went by. I believe now that it was mostly a kind of accident, mostly a lazy thing, that they didn't turn off their spotlights when they drove by the house. If I were in the cab of the truck, I'd think it was stupid to turn it off for the five seconds that we were gone past a house, I'd let it run, I'd be looking for deer and not thinking, or I'd just see the blue stutter light from the televisions inside all the houses, and I wouldn't know how the spotlight would invade them. It would not occur to me, even mildly. I would not lose any sleep about it either.

But inside the house, when they drove by with their skimming lights, for a second it would shine up the whole room from the top to bottom corners with a broad eye that roved and got to showing all the fingerprints and scratches on the window glass so it had halos sketched around it in white lines. It felt, it felt to me, exactly what I imagined it would feel like to be in a dollhouse and seen by the accosting huge eye of a giant. I froze always. And took to feeling my fists against my thighs, just wherever I was feeling them, but to stay still, because I knew in those moments that maybe someone was seeing me.

That was itself bad enough. It happened maybe once a night, usually during the evening radio news, while a bored British woman intoned about sanctions, sanctions, sanctions in a voice that sounded like it lived in a lemon. But what was worse, what started happening, was the trucks would slow down and look, actually look into the room. I could tell they were looking because they moved the spotlight from side to side. It roved, like to trace a moth through the air. And my skin chilled and I got so angry I could shoot something myself.

The second thing that happened was I had been reading the book called *Wuthering Heights*, and I had been reading the book called *Valley of the Dolls*, and I had been reading the book called *Man and His Symbols*, and I had been reading the book called *Steppenwolf*. I had not seen any books meant to be read by adults before. Even in school, we had only versions of adult things. They had been summarized and abridged since we could not be trusted to glean anything but the fattest seeds of wisdom from them, and even for those we were not much hungry. I had thought a book was for telling you something obvious: Old people are sad, children are in trouble, your mom loves you, the big evil is out there in the woods watching. I had never read a book that seemed to be able to imagine me reading it. The sentences led down into a warren of blind white paths, which shifted as I traced them, because I traced them. I was the big evil, the watcher in the woods. I was the roving bright eye casting into their rooms and seeing the merciless everything, the pouring scumming glitter of mink coats and chilblains and hidden diaries. It was romance, as I have said.

The third thing that happened was a phone call. I had thought Bernadette was out checking Mondo for ticks on the front porch—it had stayed warm the winter before and none of them had properly died off. We kept finding them on his ears and his butt, big as coffee beans and a sick gray, a swollen color. But actually, she was hunkered down in the kitchen looking for a jar of saffron threads, and before I could stop her, she picked up the phone.

"Bernadette Satterwhite," she said, "who's this?" And after a pause, she said, "What sort of nonsense is that? Jude is right here."

That could have been the end of it all, right there. I was terrified the detectives, if they ever talked with her directly, might send someone to check on Bernadette, or put her in a hospital. I ran upstairs to plug in the second phone, which I had hidden in a closet under a rag rug. I picked up the receiver and shushed my breath with a hand over my mouth.

"Are you listening?" a voice said. It was harsh from holding itself so quiet. My heart spiked itself right out of my body. "I'm in Cavetown, Maryland. His name is Richard Klink. It's a white house with a white barn. I don't know the road. The mailbox is on a green post. I'm on the second floor. I can hear horses, like, hear them running—hello? Hello?"

"I don't know what kind of foolishness amuses you," Bernadette said, "but my daughter is right here in my house." But I knew it was Jude.

"I'm so sorry. Mom. I'm sorry, I'm sorry, I'm sorry."

"What?"

"Mom, it's me. You need to write this down and call the police."

"I don't need to do a single thing. I suppose this is one of those scams."

"OK, OK, you got me. I'm just upstairs, and I thought it would be funny, Mom. To call you. I'm sorry. It wasn't very funny."

"I'll say."

"But, let's play a game? OK? Write it down like it's a story, and tell it to Dad. OK? It's a game, right? OK. He's keeping me on the second floor. I'm sure he has a gun, I don't know. The sun rises from across the road. I can hear the horses—"

"Well, come downstairs this minute. I can't find the saffron for the life of me!" And she hung up.

I half expected the phone to start ringing again right away, then realized I was listening to the dial tone.

When I went downstairs, Bernadette again had her head in the spice cabinet.

"Really, Jude, you're a little old to play tricks on your poor old mother. And to say you'd been kidnapped! A dead giveaway, my dear. How very morbid. I think you've been reading too much of Gogol, too much entirely."

"Sorry," I mumbled, and ran outside to brace myself on the chill.

I never intended to keep this information to myself. I didn't have some kind of plan. Like most evil, I suppose, mine was only a hurt hiding in whatever materials were near. My hurt had no imagination for other people. Other people, Jude, Bernadette, whoever, were about an inch deep at best, but I went on for miles. And maybe this is why, as I stood there blowing frost clouds, my thoughts began to say: *Well, you don't know it's*

Jude for sure. Why wouldn't she call 911? Maybe it was just a joke, and if it was a joke, wouldn't you feel dumb to destroy all these comforts? For no reason? And besides, besides, it's not like you did anything but overhear a conversation. In fact, most would agree that the polite thing to do when you overhear a conversation is to pretend that you didn't.

The next night we watched *Sunset Boulevard*, and Bernadette painted my toenails green. I started to get a bad feeling. I knew why. I wasn't a fool. The phone call had surfaced in my mind in a sudden flashing stab, and my shame was so great that I was panting.

"Can we stop the movie?"

"Honey, you know this is my favorite part." Gloria Swanson was holding the gun to her heart, chasing William Holden down the huge staircase, and *no one ever leaves a star.*

"But this—"

"Pipe down, for godsakes!" She held her face in her hands as if she didn't know he would slap into the pool with the bullets in his back, but really we watched the movie all the time. Once it was over, she was petting my hair and telling me the lazy truth about how life is all flaw, and it's what lets us love one another, and I felt too narcotically happy to even speak.

XVI

After the phone call, the shine fell out of things. We woke up into a winter that turned my toes white and made the hiss of the stars sound very threatening and personal. Well, we were both drinking. It was out in the open. She liked to pour a drop of raw gin in her tea. I just drank it with an ice cube in it, in little stabs at first, and then it went down like water. Sometimes I would remember Jude's phone call in a panic, but it was easy to forget. My mind knew how to hide from it.

I was watching her mend a pair of army pants. Her face was vacant of history like the heads they put on coins staring out not at the human world but into the thin metal rim, which arced away over and behind them. Like that. Her face was like that. Then she stopped and the fire snarled around the new log she threw in and she saw me and laughed.

"I've got hot dog soup for dinner," Bernadette said. "My eyes are done anyway for now."

"You don't have to," I said.

"Ha."

Hot dog soup, a Bernadette signature, was a can of chicken broth with hot dogs cut up in it and a handful of cabbage cut off a withering core in the fridge, with a can of vegetables to round it out and dark brown bread heels propped along the sides.

We sat with each other and I found that I didn't want to look at anything, but the salt burned and felt warm at least. It found a cavern at least into me. My hair had dried in strange, wavering tendrils, a few that hovered away from my head no matter how I brushed them down.

She was reading in a book and she said do you want to know a story.

Sure, I said.

She said, "I was young and it was Halloween, Easter, something. They had a cider press at the farm up the road from us and we went there in church clothes to help. But children never help with such a thing. We found a stick and stripped the twigs off and used the bad apples to play baseball with in the field."

"Baseball?"

"It didn't last."

"Why?"

"The apples were smashed. And we had to get new ones."

"Oh."

"One of the apples hit me in the head. I was running the bases. I never got to do that kind of thing."

"Did it hurt?"

"Oh yes. It hurt my eye. I couldn't open it for a week. But when I could open it again, I could see other things with it."

"What kind of other things?"

"I could see who was going to call on the phone before the phone rang. I could see when something bad was going to happen before it did. I could see snow falling through space."

"Why are you telling me this?"

"I know you're not my real daughter."

I watched a little chip of ice go flying around my eye. Mondo pressed his rump against the table leg and slumped down, so he was sitting up with his hot breath fading across my knee.

"You are not my real daughter. You're an impostor. They took the real one away in the hospital and gave me you instead." I must have looked a bit shocked.

"It's OK. I don't mind. I raised you just like you were mine, and I love you."

At first, I thought she meant like she had chosen me, Cindy. Like she remembered the phone call, and she decided she would rather keep me. But I knew this could not be possible. If anything, Bernadette's memory had gotten worse. She had always milked the goats, even after I began tending them, but one day, she came to me and meekly asked if I might show her how to do it. She asked me where Aunt Gina was keeping her hair, and other mysterious things like this. If I didn't immediately understand what she was saying, she got angry and pinched the skin of her forearm, which left little red moons up and down her arms.

"I'm glad," I said. And I was. Maybe I was just as much her real daughter as Jude was. I realized she must have been saying these things to Jude for years and years. Poor Jude, I thought. Even Jude, who came right out from her body, seemed not entirely real to Bernadette. I had felt not entirely real my whole life. By the transitive property, maybe I had found my real mother.

"I'm too much swamp thunder to have a real human baby."

"Redondo Beach," I said.

"I used to sing there," she said.

"Scary place. But I hear the flowers are beautiful."

"Redondo Beach," she said. "I used to sing there." The sky was already choked with blue. It would flee when I wasn't looking. The barn lights flared a pure white like no other time of the year and reminded me of the overheads in the school gym. It seemed like lit-up fluoride. I had not been to school in a long time.

"What did you sing? In Redondo Beach?" I felt like all of my threads had been combed out and I was happy to go to sleep soon. I was not really paying attention. But Bernadette picked up her spoon with a fist wrapped around it. She brought it up to her shoulder. The muscles trembled. The handle, once she threw it, hit on the sticking-up bone of my wrist. It clattered over the edge. Mondo jumped.

"I'm so damn tired of telling you everything. Why don't you just go away?"

"I'm sorry," I said.

"It was 'La Bamba.' For the last time, my god." Then she stood up and slapped me, square on the cheek.

I didn't want to cry over it, but I was tasting the metal in my mouth, which meant that I would. They were paper, hot sand, the tears. I levered my head to hide them, but she saw and searched up into my face.

"Baby? Hey, baby? I'm sorry. I'm sorry. I shouldn't. I know I shouldn't. I should never. OK?" She pulled my hand to her chest and clamped on her heart, which was fluttering. "You feel how sorry I am?"

I didn't want to flinch but my nerves were all plucked up. She noticed. Her eyes went flat, and she slapped me again, and wailed. She stood away from the table and left the chair scudding backward. I thought she was going up to the bathroom to run cool water on her face, so I started clearing the table. But then I heard a rip in the air, and another. Bernadette cried out, or grunted, some sound with a lot of effort behind it. From the sound, I thought she was pulling down shelves from the wall.

But what I found: Bernadette had pulled her shift down over her shoulders and braced her left hand by the bathroom mirror so she could swat this little leather whip at her back. The tip must have been weighted. It sounded high-pitched and serious. Her back was bright red with raised welts like what I remembered from giving myself eraser burns in school. It's funny, how you realize a mystery the moment you solve it: The welts on Bernadette's arms, the welts Jude had said were just color guard hazing. And of course, the day when she caught me smoking. She wouldn't look at me, though I was sure she could see me over her shoulder in the mirror. I approached, and put my hand, careful and slow but very heavy, upon her right shoulder.

"Hey, Bernadette," I said. "Can I see that?"

She handed it to me. Her jaw hung slack.

"Thank you," I said. I marched off to hide it. And trusted she'd pull herself together.

I got rid of the dinner dishes. I poured all the hot dog soup into a bowl for Mondo, but he had too much sense to eat food that had been slapped over. Instead he pressed his nose into the backs of my knees while I washed out the saucepan. Why didn't I go home? I don't know. I don't know. Maybe I thought this was home, always, eventually. I thought home always turned into this.

XVII

All the goats were inside except for one. Panda Jane lay down and got back up. She was usually so friendly with me I had to watch I didn't trip on her. Some stuff was coming out of her butt, under her tail. There was a long string of it, milky-sick like snot. Some brown and red threads were in it, and I had of course to realize that it must be an emergency, because it was blood. It had snowed all the failing night before and was not done yet. The yard and goat pens looked strange, like the ground had been turned to glass underneath.

It could be anyone has the arm of salvation within them. It is an extra arm, the arm of salvation, and not like the bony scrabble of the flesh. It comes from the chest. It leans out and opens. The hand holds on to things, mostly people. It holds on the cleft of the ribs.

It was a bad day. All day we'd been fighting about what time of winter it was. Bernadette would say it was cold today, but we were lucky we'd had such a warm winter. But we hadn't, at all. The pipes froze four times and eventually I rigged up a lawn chair over a bucket instead of using the toilet. We had some long snows when the delivery boy from Bell's Grocery couldn't get through. Things were getting so unreliable. We ate crackers and drank broth.

Bernadette had her feet laid out on the table and was flexing her toes. One of the brand-new barn kittens marched over her stomach and fell off the other side. Outside, Panda Jane was still off by herself yelling.

"I think something is wrong with her. With Panda Jane."

"Sweetie, I looked at her yesterday."

"You should see her right now."

We stood at the side window. Panda Jane had her forehooves up on a tree stump. She was staring up into the sky, like she was waiting for instructions.

"She's stargazing," Bernadette said. "They do it when they're about to kid." She lay across the couch and drummed her fingers on her chest bones, on the kitten.

"Aren't you going to do something?"

"Something? About what?"

"About Panda Jane."

"Oh, sweetie. All the goats died. They all died. The fire took them away."

I called Doctor Vic, the veterinarian. Bernadette had his home number written on the back of a phone bill. He sounded like he was talking from the bottom of a well.

"Yep?"

"Hello. I'm calling from Bernadette's. I've got a pregnant goat here that is having its baby," I said.

"Yeah, and what?"

"I don't know, I don't know what to do."

"Bernie's delivered a shit ton of goats. She knows what she's doing." As he said this, Bernadette was blowing an eiderdown feather up and up into the air like a child.

"Please," I said. "She can't do it right now."

"Who *is* this anyway?"

"This is—Jude." I couldn't break the spell, not with Bernadette sitting right there in front of me.

"That is not a thing to be joking about," he said. "Whoever you are."

"Please, I don't know about goats. Please just help me."

"I don't truck with pranksters. Now bye."

My boots were still wet from earlier when I had been out shoveling the drive and digging out the pickup. My socks were dark around the toes, but I'd picked up a confetti of straw and rock salt walking around in the kitchen with the cord springing and winding around the chairs. In all the prairie movies I had ever seen, you had to boil a tub of water whenever something was being born. If no one would help me, I was determined to handle things myself. I started a pan going over the back burner and held my hands over it, watched the first heat shimmer up and roll over the surface.

"Get me those blankets from upstairs," I said to Bernadette. She had her eyes closed with the feather between them.

"Oh, the princess shall have blankets, many blankets may she have," she said.

"Not for me. The goat's having a baby right now. Like, right this second."

She heaved away and went up the stairs with her long skirt trailing after her, huffing like a teenager.

The panic was all in my hands, which was good, because I could send them out away from me to do tasks and not think and not let the worry cramp up into my stomach where it could make me dizzy, trail against the walls, feel hollow, or retch. I started coffee also. The sky was getting blue already. That long light was coming through the sky, the last we would see for the night, although it was barely really four in the afternoon.

The goats lived in a little lean-to. It was really just a woodshed with some walls tacked on. The space was shallow, maybe four foot wide. They were threaded together in long lines for warmth but hardly any space to move. The air smelled like dust and jam. Panda Jane was not there, though she had been in the corner when I had checked them before and broke the ice on their water troughs.

Snow blew off the roof in a fierce glittering wave and settled again over the trees. I was grateful it was deep at least, so I could follow her tracks, although I heard her soon enough yelling out in the middle of the hawthorn waste. I hadn't brought a light with me. I thought it would do to see the slim light off the snow blaring up from the ground. We were moon people, we had been moon people all along, we could see in the dark like a spell.

The mucus plug had fallen down through the snow because it had still been warm when she dropped it. I had to scan all sideways with my hands flatted to find it. She didn't want me near her. She lay down and got up again, lay down and got up. The hawthorn scrub made a low dark room where I couldn't get at her at all. It would have to be good enough. She yelled in bursts like a siren, then got tired out, got up, and squatted out a little pee.

Inside, Bernadette had forgotten about the blankets. When I called out for her, she came a few steps down the stairs and leaned her head across to see me.

"Hey, come on," I said. "You better get your boots on. I don't know what to do but I need help."

Bernadette had been wearing a fanny pack around the house. It was simplest to get all her things that way, the things she was always asking for. I didn't understand it. The salt shaker, a quartz crystal, a blackened quarter, a torn-up king from a playing card are what she had in there. In thinking, she'd let her fingers droop into the pouch and run over the things she carried as if their edges might help her to remember what was going on.

"But the birth man already came, sugar. He's been and gone, and took all the little lambies to heaven."

I walked out of her vision and put my forehead against the pebbled white run of the refrigerator. If I counted fifteen I could try again. This was the way it worked the best sometimes, when I couldn't get her to agree. She still forgot, but was less embarrassed around me. Since I'd been living full time in the house, I got to be a part of the scenery that she would revise and tint with good lights.

I turned back around the corner. She had sat at the top of the stairs with her knees widing out her skirt between them, a valley. She took out her things from the fanny pack and rested them there, put them back in an order I would never make sense of.

"Come on, Mom. I want to show you the moon! Put your boots on. The moon is really, really beautiful tonight."

"Oh no you don't," she said. "I've fallen for the old 'come see the moon' trick. Never again, my dear."

I grabbed the keys to the truck and pulled it up to the copse where Panda Jane had hidden herself so I could run the headlights in there to see. I didn't really know how to drive, but my hand slid the gear shift around like it had become an expert without me. I crawled in and tore up marks in the mud. Panda Jane had her hooves back up on the stump, straining her head up. She panted and looked at the moon. Nothing was coming out of her except a clear globe of stuff. It looked like a water balloon with veins on the outside. I still had the mucus plug in my pocket. All the slime had rubbed off. It looked like a small, clear cake of soap but there were red streaks in it. I pushed it around in my palm. The blood looked wrong.

The headlights blinked as the truck shifted up and down in its idle. Some foam was crusting her lips. It seemed like she had been trying a long time.

I didn't know much about animals. Some girls raised up calves from a bottle and like that, and would probably know what to do. We Stoats are not known for husbandry, though. We never had anything stranger than a dog, except for the brief, doomed chickens which Blond You and Black You eventually terrorized into extinction.

In a back corner, between books on macrobiotic cookery and Vedic chanting, I found a volume called *Raising Milk Goats the Modern Way.* The pages were tea color and stiff from being shut for so long, and Jude had once drawn big scribble-faced cats across the table of contents. The birthing chapter was surprisingly casual. "Goats have been reproducing without human help for millennia!" it correctly claimed. And yet it also included many grim drawings of a person pulling limp baby goats out of their mothers.

Bernadette had draped herself across the captain's chair by the wood stove and was passing her dreaming hand through the place where heat lines shimmered. She had put on a Nina Simone record.

"Don't you sometimes think all the good ones are dead?" she said. "Because I do. I really, really do." She sounded drunk—it was a drunk idea even if she wasn't slurring. But I had no time for that. I started running the tap and then pulled my arm through the sweatshirt sleeve. The water steamed. I didn't feel anything but bright where I ran the soap over my elbow and shoulder. It was a useful feeling, satisfying in spite of the crisis.

"That's a funny way to take a bath, baby. À la carte."

"Panda Jane is kidding right now. If you'd care to join me. I really, really need your help."

"*You're* kidding. Ha! Ha." Just like that, she was peeling an orange.

Outside, I clamped the book open under my knee and bent my jaw open to hold the flashlight in my teeth. I flipped to the picture that looked like the way Panda Jane was standing and read: "If breech birth is suspected, manually observe the orientation of the skull before pulling (by leg or shoulder)." I hesitated. Panda Jane was still yelling. But she was already hurting, I reasoned. I only hoped I didn't hurt her more.

I put my hand up in her a ways and was shocked to find it had wrapped itself on a skull. I thought I could feel the kid's eyes shivering in the sockets.

I stood still a moment. It seemed like a plain impossible thing. I wanted to just not exist. I had nothing. Children have no things they can say. So I leaned down into the dark where the roots were diving into the pale mud and the stars ticking away overhead, and maybe I prayed in my heart. I loved Panda Jane. I loved all the goats. I knew Bernadette loved them, too. And I was pretending to be Jude, who was good and brave, much more than myself. I was such a coward I couldn't even see around the hurt. But I could try at least to do this right.

I pushed past the skull this time, my hand starfishing. It felt like the inside of a mouth. I said every sweet thing to her. I said she was beautiful, I loved her. I cried into my collar and watched as her breathing got wet and the strain made her back leg shake. She was bearing down on the front legs hoisting into the stump and for nothing, for nothing. But then I caught the hard curve of a hoof and walked my fingers up to find the knee joint and the shoulder. Panda Jane gagged on her cries and resumed.

I pulled on it just a little ways and felt nothing change. It wasn't coming. I looked again in the book: "Be careful to work with the goat's rhythms, not against. Nevertheless, it may be necessary to pull with some force," it said. There were no other suggestions.

I tried again. I pulled so hard I thought I would yank the leg clean off. Panda Jane was yelling unbroken. God, how she hated me. I felt the leg squirm in the fluids. My arm burned. I held around her hips to brace me. We were murdering each other. I pulled the murder out. She shouted it. We were busy alive in the blood of that moment that stretched out and took over the sky and was bigger than any I had known.

When I fell back onto my butt I thought my hand must have slipped, but the baby goat was there in my lap, about the size of my boot and glossed in yellow crud. I had crushed it or killed it, I was sure, but then its legs began slowly swimming. I put it down in my sweater, against my skin.

Panda Jane had lain on her side, and a little leg hooked its way out. There was another one. I was delirious and overheated. My mouth tasted strange.

But the second goat slipped out like nothing and Panda Jane licked at its yellow goo. Her placenta wobbled nearby like a moon drop.

I got on my feet, then stepped up into the cab to turn the truck off. I rested a minute with my hands on the roof. My face was wet. I was crying.

And I knew this also: I was a luxury of blood. That's how it felt, how good. I moved them into the lean-to. It seemed wrong to leave them outside, but the book actually cautioned against bringing newborn goats into the house, so I knew I wasn't the first to think this thought.

"Happy birthday," I said to the goats, or perhaps to the night, or perhaps to the things of the world in general.

I hollered toward the house that Bernadette should come see. I saw her shadow move through the yellow light inside. But a big band record started up instead, and I watched her waltz alone. So I lay on my stomach and watched the goats. I named them: Butter and Dirtbike. But the cold seeped into my shoulders. And I felt a burn of cold in my chest. When I went inside, Bernadette had gone upstairs. The record spun on static. But her bottle was still on the table, and when I pulled on it, something clicked open in my chest. It felt like someone had just pulled a knot loose in my gut. I drank again and some gin ran from the corner of my mouth. I tipped some of it into a mug. It laughed as I poured it, and me, too, I laughed. Happy birthday. And sat again outside to drink it under the stars, which plowed across the scrub of the sky, watery and glorious.

This one I heard from Melda, long after the whole business was over and I had returned, more or less, to my life. Melda's mom, Darienne, worked in the Greene County Sheriff's Office, and had seen the fake Jude incident herself. The fake Jude selected a *People* magazine from the cubby, and looked rather unremarkable at first. She had highlighted blond hair and a pink gloss on her lips. She didn't remove her parka or unzip it, and from her purse she brought out little pony bottles of water and a bag of trail mix. It didn't seem like this was her first time waiting for someone's arraignment or bench warrant or whatever it was to get cleared up, so Darienne left her alone. With glum discipline, the woman removed a foot-long hoagie from her purse and dispatched it in swift, scarcely chewed bites, cutting her eyes up to the TV bolted to the ceiling, which typically played a PSA about getting your cholesterol checked. She sorted apart trail mix on the particleboard table, and with the raisins she formed a cross. She was humming something patriotic, the "Battle Hymn of the Republic," maybe. She kept bothering the other waiting-room people, asking if they knew what an ego death is, and what are the signs.

"Can I help you?" Darienne asked at last.

"Why, yes," the woman said. "I'm here about a missing-persons case. Jude Vanderjohn."

"OK. Do you have information for a detective, or something like that?"

"Something like that," the woman said. She had a deep chuckle. "You see, I'm Jude Vanderjohn. I'm not missing anymore. You can stop looking for me."

No fool, that Darienne. She led the woman to an interview room, and locked her in. By the time Detective Torboli arrived, the woman was beginning to protest her treatment by singing "We Shall Overcome," stamping her loafers upon the linoleum and holding both fists in the air.

According to her driver's license, she was Jeanette Rush of Crucible, Pennsylvania, not that she was tricking anyone anyway. Jeanette Rush was strictly Caucasian and middle-aged, no matter what she said to the contrary. She told Detective Torboli she had been abducted by "a big black buck" and made to do "un-Christian things," which she described with uninterruptible zeal. As she made her litany, the detective flexed his toes in his shoes, a strategy he adopted for retaining a sense of the real when it was otherwise hard to come by.

"I suppose you can just give the reward money to me now," she said. "Haha!"

"I'm the missing black girl," she also said.

"It's been so hard for me," she also said. "I'm weary to my heart."

XVIII

I had been folding paper cranes in Bernadette's bed when the car pulled up. It was Christmas Eve, but we weren't going to do anything to celebrate that night because she thought it was Christmas every few days, and I was feeling a little bit fat from all the toffee. At first, I thought maybe the car was someone's relatives lost without their GPS. In the country, unexpectedly pulling your car up in front of someone's house is almost as invasive as walking right in and helping yourself to a plate of dinner. I crouched by the window. Alistair wore a duster coat. His wheeled suitcase stuttered behind him in the snow and gravel. He doubled back with a crate of wine and a turkey. He pulled one of the bottles from the crate and presented it to Bernadette. *"Beaujolais!"* she said. It sounded like a salutation or a blessing. She cooed over the bottle like it was a newborn.

I had never expected Alistair to come back. Didn't he know we had a whole world without him? To me, it was just simply not a thing fathers would do. I had never seen my own father, for example. Once, he called the house and I picked up. He said, "Oh. Oh shit," and asked me to get my mother.

Going by the notes of their voices, Alistair and Bernadette were happy to see each other. It was like their last fight had never happened—and for Bernadette, I guess it hadn't. For the first time, I considered the possibility that Bernadette's forgetfulness made things easy for people other than myself.

This was obviously no afternoon drop-in. My mind fizzed. Even if I stayed, I would have to excuse myself eventually or explain the whole arrangement to him. And if I stayed, I had no idea what sort of things Bernadette might say or do.

I wrapped myself up in the warmest things I could find—a fur coat, an oxblood sweater, and mudded-up Walmart snow boots—and went out the back door and into the twilight. Toward home, because I really didn't have anywhere else to go. I believe Alistair saw me slipping away, but I didn't care, and couldn't think of a better idea.

My muscles were getting tough from all the farm chores. I picked my way up the hill with only a little sweat freezing on my scalp. Part of me felt very sorry for myself, and part of me enjoyed the romance of sudden exile—*alone, in the woods, on Christmas!* It sounded sorrowful in the exact way I liked. I couldn't remember why I had ever been afraid to walk in the woods at night. It was all creatures, and I was a creature. Everything was legal between me and the rest.

And maybe, although I would not have said so at the time, it felt a little beautiful to go out in the world without trying to hold my face a certain way and act how I thought Jude would act. I was empty of all that. It felt good breathing, and gaining the top of the hill I started to recognize little places in the woods where I had played, like the tree I liked to climb and the ledges where mosses drooled down underneath. My favorite pretend game was being a sea monster, and the rush of trees in the wind crashing like waves. Myself! I didn't mind it. Now that I was in our woods again, I felt like I had come a long way. When I stopped and turned back, the lights at Bernadette's were still near, but small enough that I could wink them out with my thumb.

I heard the music before I crested the hill. Just a far-off small music with voices in it and all like that. Party sounds, whatever those are. I'm sure you know them. Why are they always the same? Every party I've watched from the outside has sounded like the people inside had turned into music. I wondered if Clinton had the TV turned all the way up, watching some black-and-white movie.

But in fact it was an actual party. I saw it all in the yellow squares of the windows. Clinton held a shot glass up to Shayna's lips and goosed her in the ribs as she tipped her head back to take it so the tequila went all down her shirt. Blond You and Black You were inside the house, which was unusual, and they were playing a little rough, busting into the table legs, trying to get at the ham. There was an astonishing amount of food on the table, though it looked like they'd already been eating it a long time. And in the middle, my mother. My mother, with a yellow paper crown slipped down over one eye. The lamp burned over her head. She ate up all the light in the room.

"Oh *shit*," Clinton said.

"Oh my *god*," my mother said.

Shayna poked at my blond roots with a clammy fingertip. "Wow. You should let me touch you up. Although I gotta say, it's a look."

No one had gotten up until Shayna pulled off my coat and rubbed her hands all over my shoulders to warm me. Then my mother came and hugged me hard against her. She had to reach up a little. Had she always been this small? She had one of those hairdos that looked like clouds, and I could tell she had just dyed it because the fuzz hairs at her temples were vivid, the way they aren't in nature, and even though it was winter she was wearing shorts and little high-heeled bronze sandals. She looked fine, perfect, wonderful. She looked like something was wrong with me. I closed my eyes and some tears melted out, although I didn't mean or want them to. She smelled, as always, like bread, copper, and hair spray.

"My only, only, only," she said. "Baby girl, oh, I missed you. Let's make you a plate. You look skinny!" Clinton made a face like: That's not skinny. And I wasn't. I actually never was. I was embarrassed for Mom, the way she tried to flatter me.

But she put together some ham pieces with globes of fat on their ends, and scraped up mashed potatoes, scummy green beans, and Jell-O salad from the bowls. I was trying to tell how long she had been back based on the housekeeping. I guessed at least a week: The moldings gleamed and the windows were mirrory, without the feathered fingerprints we left from poking out at the world. Even the junk mail had been stacked in a wicker basket under the table.

"Where's Virgil?" I said. They stopped. Everyone looked to Mom.

"Well, honey," my mother said, "he's in jail." Her eyebrows were all the way up. She looked at me like my asking was more outrageous than what she had just said. "Or didn't you know?"

"He's in jail?"

"He's been in, shit, two months?" Clinton said. "Thought you'd've heard. Everybody was talking about it. It was after they found that girl's wallet. It's all bullshit, of course. Everybody knows what she was up to." Shayna skimmed her eyes away to the ceiling.

"How was I supposed to hear about that?" My mother rolled her eyes and snapped the ash off her cigarette. The ashtray was full of them, Camel lights with wet pink gloss on the ends. "And when did you get back, anyway?" I asked her. "Why didn't you tell me?"

Clinton answered for her: "You was the one who left."

"Why didn't you tell me Mom was back?"

Clinton held up his palms like: You got me. He shrugged.

A glacier built around the moment. And then I sat down. I ate the food because I couldn't think of a single other thing to do. I sank down through my own water. It closed up over my head and down I went. They were on talking about something else. The longwall mine broke the water table under Duke Lake, which had become a field of mud. Someone was arsoning cars on the back roads around Hundred. Edna Mae's house was full of snakes, and she wouldn't let anybody in to help. Somebody sang a bad anthem at the Super Bowl, and people got fat, and I had forgotten it was like this. Always, always, always. No matter the event, talk would flood over it and hurl it away. Bernadette's was also flooded with talk, but it was different. We named where our feelings lay in our bodies, and were they: heavy, feathery, choking, chilly, staticky, thrumming. Name it, she told me, and it won't own your ass. Just then my mother was talking about a diet in *Parade* magazine where you pray over your food to bar the calories' entrance. I dropped my eyes under the table. I was ashamed of something I didn't quite understand at that time, which was: My mother was not very smart. It wasn't just that she had never heard of Tintoretto, because who gives a shit about that? But there was some flavor of stillness in her gaze. She did not see any worlds beneath this one. This was a rude new understanding, and I did not care for it at all.

That's when I noticed the baby. It was sat in its car seat on the floor in the kitchen like groceries someone had forgotten to put up. Also, nobody was talking to it or looking at it. It was Mom's, I knew right away, although I couldn't say how. The baby looked like it had been carved out of a potato, except for the motion in its face.

When it was time for presents, we moved along to the living room, which had gone chilly from being empty, the way rooms do in winter. Clinton got Mom a shrink-wrapped basket of lotions packed in red crinkle paper. Shayna got her a trio of jewel-tone nail polishes. Mom had new binoculars for Clinton, grippy socks and scratchers for Shayna. I liked the names. Cash Time. King of Cash. Buckets of Cash. Wild Cherries. I didn't understand that there was no present for me at first. "You girls can share," my mother said when she caught me eyeing the lottery tickets. I looked around, and everybody inspected their hands. The air fell apart. I wondered if we might address this awkwardness, but Mom only sighed, smacked the tops of her thighs, and walked off to skim a little more tequila out of the bottle. Shayna whispered, "*My present to you is a makeover, you goober freak.*"

The rest of the day we tried to scoot into formations with each other, but it was hard. I sat and investigated the baby. When I put a finger on his forehead, it left a white mark for a moment, before the blood rushed back in.

I snuck away to my bedroom, but it had withered somewhat, a dried-out place. I could not believe how carelessly I had left my broken-necked doll there in the dark. She was flung into the corner, in a pose of cartoon despair. I held her to me and tried to warm the aloneness out of her, but she stayed cold against my chest. At that moment, Virgil was in a brick room called a jail. I wondered, for some reason, what he would do if he caught a cold in there. Did they give you tissues? And I imagined my brother pinching the top of his nose, looking up at the ceiling, where I was watching him. I swear he saw me, and it was the real thing. His eyes were wet. And mine, too. Mine, too. I was crying.

Most of the time, my mind knew I was doing something wrong by being Jude, but I didn't usually allow my whole self to know. At Bernadette's, everything was easy. If my mind got loud, all I had to do was ask about Redondo Beach and off she'd go. Once, I hurt Bernadette's feelings by spitting out a bite of pancake—there was a thumbtack in it, to be fair, but she was much insulted all the same. All I had to do was leave the room and wait thirty seconds. When I came back, well, hello honey lamb, and where have you been? None of that worked here. I knew I could get Virgil out of jail if I told the truth about the phone call. And I also knew I could not tell the truth. I was too miserable about myself, too afraid to show what I had done. The feeling tilted upon itself and began to spin, and I could not allow it to pick up speed, to pick me up and fling me. I slammed the door and went to wash the dinner dishes because I didn't want to show that my hands were shaking.

While I washed up, Mom and Clinton and Shayna watched a kid movie on television. It was about a girl and an orphaned dog. Mom and Clinton passed a bag of pork rinds between them and if they felt any distress for the girl or the dog, it was not breaking the surface. The TV was new, and so large that it felt like it was trying to engulf you, which they enjoyed.

By the time I was done, Clinton had changed the channel to some old football game. Shayna pulled me onto the couch and shared her blanket. Nobody was saying anything about the baby, about Virgil, about where did I get a fur coat even. About Bernadette, about Jude, about the numbness in your belly that lets you eat until you disappear. The crowd in the background of the game was like a snow of sound. I believe the football drone should be made a medicine, if anything should be made a medicine. I know I would take it every day, if it was a pill.

I stayed for three days. Shayna and I saw the talk shows. I let her fix my roots. We bundled up to walk to Pecjak's for something to do. Mom was into making chili "Texas style," which only meant she simmered it until it was dark like a scab. That's where she had been, apparently. Texas. The baby's name was Wade. I thought that was just the most bedoomed name I had ever heard. Wade stayed in his car seat in the kitchen most of the day. As if by fairy magic, I knew not to pick him up or chatter at him. I know that sounds cold, but I figured I had got through it myself, and he would have to do the same.

My eyes bent in a weird way without Jude's glasses, which I had hidden in my coat pocket. I tried to slip back into being Cindy, but I wasn't sure I remembered the right way to do it. Wasn't I a sloucher? Didn't I play with my fingers and mumble, or was I remembering this all wrong? I sassed back at Shayna so much she started calling me fireball, but not in a mean way and it felt nice.

From our back fence I could see down to Bernadette's house. Over the day, I spied from there so often Mom thought I was sneaking cigarettes, and said I might as well smoke honestly. So I smoked, too, and prayed my eyes down into the valley to disappear Alistair's car. When it was finally gone and stayed gone for a few hours, I chanced it and went down into the woods. I didn't say a word of good-bye to my family.

I picked up a stack of cordwood on my way into the house. I wanted it to look like I'd been working outside all morning, long enough that she might have forgotten the interruption in our routine. It had occurred to me that, with a few solid days in the house, Alistair could have finally convinced her that Jude was missing, and my magic might be over. My hope was to slip back into the rhythm of things without rippling the surface—if I made my presence quiet for most of the afternoon, I figured I'd be safe. I waltzed in and took care to stoke the stove and stack the wood without speaking, just like I would on an ordinary day. The house smelled wrong, like milk in the back of a mouth. Bernadette wore an entirely new outfit: tufted slippers, a fuzzy purple sweater, wide-legged pants of black silk. A pouch of her belly leaped out over the waistband. Her cheeks and nose were bright red. She didn't look up.

There wasn't much visible evidence of Alistair. He had forgotten a razor on the sink, was all. But I detected a new note in the silence. There was some sulk in it, like waiting for the other person to apologize. I found all twelve bottles of wine empty and rinsed clean in a way that seemed a little self-righteous. I guessed they had ended with a fight. Trash had spilled out the top of the can and again, somehow, there were dirty dishes in the oven.

"Baby, hurry. We've got to get started if we're going to make it through this box set! Get in here."

"Box set?" I hoped if I began talking from offstage it would help me come slowly into focus again.

"This William Holden box set you got me. Come on, you said. You said we would watch it today and tomorrow and tomorrow. And where are the horsetails?"

"What horsetails?" And what were horsetails, I wondered.

"The ones you said you'd get for my tea." I propped myself in the doorway. "Oh god, don't tell me you forgot." She clucked at me and moved aside on the couch so I could position myself for what turned out to be *Invisible Stripes*. Alistair must have gotten it for her. Bernadette petted my shoulders like always, but I got an itch on me like I was going to shake apart if she kept touching me like that. I shrugged her off the way a horse shrugs off flies. But her hand was back again a moment later. I tried to sit through, but she kept rubbing the same circle on my shoulder, and the spot got warm and irritated. There was something needy about it. I shook her off again. She resettled her hand right away.

"Mom, stop it."

"Hmm? Whatever you say, sweetie lamb." And then, as if it had just occurred to her, she dropped her hand on my shoulder and traced the same circle again. I pinned my jaw in and tried not to flinch. How had my mother been back a whole week and not sent for me? My mother? How come nobody told me about Virgil? I always became a mind reader when I was sad, so I could hear it just then, how Clinton must have told Mom I was spoiled and thought myself better than them all of a sudden, gone down the road to listen to operas and eat figs, whatever I imagined him imagining me doing, except did Clinton even know what figs were, I couldn't be certain. Would he have thought opera? He wouldn't. But it was true. Bernadette put vinegar and black pepper on figs, and I liked them that way. I adopted the opinion that *Nessun Dorma* was beautiful and to hell with what it meant.

I had started to think that all the emptiness I saw in things was not bad but a holy place. Maybe it was fucked up that I couldn't give myself permission to think that kind of thing unless I was being this slippery person I invented who could disappear in so many ways and yet feel more solid than my disappearing self, and who was the opposite of the real Jude, who was also gone. Who was in danger. And then I thought again of the phone call. I petted and nursed all my reasons: It wasn't my business. Jude had meant to call her mother, and that's what she got. It wasn't my fault that her mother was impossible.

My shoulder felt red and stinging in the place where Bernadette kept tracing on it. Anyone who looked at us would assume that she was comforting me, but it was a comfort I didn't want. It burned. I fought myself to stay there under her hand, and bit my lip to keep from flinching away. The moment the movie was over, I jumped up to turn off the TV. A white repeating line skipped left to right across the screen.

"Oh, don't turn it off! I love this part," Bernadette said. "Oh, it's just so sad and so true."

Jude's room felt haunted that night. Oh, listen to me: I was haunted that night, but I always attribute my moods to the air. On the pillow, someone had left a box papered in blue and gold. I opened the card: *JUDE*. I hadn't even let myself know how much it hurt to watch my family opening presents without me, and it all came out just then. My throat tied itself up. It didn't even occur to me that this gift might be for the real Jude, and not me. I didn't recognize Alistair's handwriting, and why would I?

I lifted out a hand-painted bowl. Inside, cats, goats, and rabbits danced around the sun. On the outer rim, a night sky prickled with stars. There was a note wrapped in pink tissue, which I also opened.

Dear daughter:

Do you know the definition of faith? I thought I did. For all my life I have served the idea that faith and hope are continuous. Recent events have persuaded me to visit the dictionary, however. Suffering makes familiar words taste strange, I suppose. In any case, I found that faith is defined as "possessing a complete certainty," or in some variants, "acting upon a complete certainty." It occurs to me, truly, how tremendous a task that is for us here on Earth. I don't know how to do it. I am prey to superstition and misery. I have told others that if they could get quiet enough, they would hear within themselves the voice of the eternal, and all would be peace with them. I had no idea what I was asking them to do. In fact, I am ashamed that I ever considered myself qualified to give such advice. Only now have I become truly qualified: My heart is broken. I am listening for the eternal. I seem to think that if I bring you this gift, you will have to come home and receive it. Maybe I'm a fool, but maybe, in fact, you will. Maybe you will read these words. I hold the thread of that moment lightly in my hands, even though hope is a little less than "complete certainty." But in writing this, I am perhaps keeping a part of you alive: The part of you that reads it. Here is my certainty. I know that giving thanks proves God's presence—otherwise, there is no one to thank. Please, enjoy this gift. It reminded me of your favorite story (the rabbits).

Love, Papa

The shame rode me around the room. I hung somewhere just outside of myself, crying for all of time. I saw Virgil looking up to a sign in the blue. I saw him drawing a cross against the bare sky, just a little one with his pinkie. I didn't know what it meant, except that it was a warning. Everything saw me. All of this world is a witness. I put the bowl away in the closet, under heaped clothes. It seemed to hum in my mind, in a way I couldn't stop hearing. The letter, too. I hid them away so they couldn't see me. And still, I felt the eyes of them gleaming from the dark.

XIX

It was a warm, strange day. The sun was on my shoulders and I felt confused about it before I figured out what it was. I had thought it was some sort of mammal landed on me, flung out of the sky.

I stood by the window and watched an icicle with the sun pouring through it. It went bright as an arc flame. I made it a game—I burned my eyes on it, then brought the roving purple spot around the valley, tracing the places where the hills and sky met. In the yard, the goats roamed in a circle. Wide, though they could not get out of it. Ann Richards went toward the road and skirted there with her head pinned hard against her shoulder. The other goats were walking like that, too. They were coming over the lawn, on the long rip of snow the wind had carved up ornamentally.

Bernadette was pickling gooseberries—where had she gotten these gooseberries?—and the pink pepper fumed up into the air and the vinegar was like a bolt thrown through my nose. She was horribly, horribly drunk. I didn't even care to try and stop her anymore. She had burned her hand on the saucepan and taped a paper towel over the puffy skin. She was being impossible and I was sick of it. She had been seeing William Holden movies all over the place. I kept pulling her face out of the steaming fumes on the stove where she claimed to be watching *The Wild Bunch*. "Baby, why are you at the window? What are you watching?" she asked me.

"The goats are playing. It's—I don't know. They're waltzing. Come look."

They were still going in circles, the goats. They all had their heads wrenched down to the side. Butter and Dirtbike did tight spins like jewelry box ballerinas. They looked like people who had to pretend, for whatever reason, to be goats, but could not bring enough naturalness. They reminded me of how in cartoons, you whistle to seem innocent if you've done a bad thing, or when there's a bad thing you want to do. Dolores chased her tail again and again until she fell down. Maybe they were dancing. I really didn't know anything.

I thought Bernadette would find it funny. There was so much I thought terrible that made her laugh. She loved really terrible things. But she sank to her knees by Dolores, gentled her, pulled the goat's lower eyelid down from the eye and looked into the skin. It was white, like a sliver of eye had come off. Before I could think Bernadette ran back into the house. Dolores was vibrating, very gently, but the quiver kept her from getting up. When I went back in Bernadette had the phone off its cradle already, calling the veterinarian. She was crying. *Hurry* was all I heard. I put on a real coat. I figured it might be a long time we were outside with them, but I had no idea.

Doctor Vic pulled his truck right up on the grass and pulled on his gloves. They dimpled from the dark hairs on the backs of his hands. It was a dainty gesture. Everything that happened, I was seeing it wrong.

Doctor Vic called them together in a pen. Hey pretty, hey pretty, he said to them. Get on over here, pretty girl, right there is just fine. And took out his pen flashlight to look under their eyes, like Bernadette had. The truck was still running. He put on a sterile face mask and gave one to Bernadette. He brought out a black bag, a case from the bag, and assembled five needles on the driver's seat. They had neon green plungers. I remember because it was the only color I saw all day.

Bernadette held the goats for their shots. I tried to pet on Ann Richards, but Doctor Vic held me back with a stiff arm. I don't remember any of the things they were saying, only the tone. It was like TV voices bleeding through a motel wall. Bernadette had gloves on also. Nobody offered me any.

Again I thought to find a way to be helping by bending my body over the goats like they did. Bernadette couldn't look at me.

"Go inside," she said.

"The time for that is gone," Doctor Vic said to me. "Enough, OK?"

I wanted to be useful. I made more coffee. When there is nothing else to do, I believe somebody should make coffee. But that day, my hands had died off at the wrists and I couldn't do anything. I looked at the percolator and tried to remember its deed in all this. What part of it was a mouth, what part of it would talk to me. The radio had flown into a patch of weather static. It was all around me, the snapping fuzz of that sound. I stood still at the sink, trying to feel it. It scattered against my hair and against my throat, which was wet because I was crying again.

I filled a thermos and brought it out to them. Doctor Vic was pulling apart the round bale in the feeder with his hands. He had gone crazy, I figured. The bale was a darker brown inside, and the sun bleached the crust. But I didn't know about hay. This would sound impossible to some people, I know. The Stoats are mowers. That is all a Stoat is good for. Nobody should know hay if a Stoat does not.

"This is your problem right here," Doctor Vic said. Bernadette had taken off her gloves, but she was warming her hands on the back of her neck. She looked down into what he held. The hay was foxed through with black speckles. It was mold, although I didn't understand this until later. "This bale hasn't been properly changed for months. It's listeriosis, all of them."

"What do you think?" she asked him. They were still not looking at me. The hay was my job, and we all knew it was.

"I'm sorry," he said.

It was like somebody had put out an alert on the radio. For all I know, that's right.

The trucks pulled alongside Doctor Vic's, and when there was no more room, parked along the road with two tires hanging off the edge, where it rolled away and down to the field across from the house. They had thermoses, too, and splits of wood from their own supplies. Doctor Vic picked a spot away behind the barn, across the crick which was black, like it went down for miles. He indicated for them to lay the fires there. They passed the wood hand from hand in a chain that went up to the road. Damon Wise, Buddy Metheny, Marlon Whipkey, Asa Gehoe, Mark and Wyatt Tedrow. Even Clinton. He looked like anyone I didn't know. If he saw me, he didn't signal it.

They were not all men. There was Janice Creekmur in tan coveralls with her hair clipped to the plastic band of a ball cap and Shauna Minor in just a flannel jacket, smoking a cigarette hung from her lip. Their cheeks were planed in shadow and their lips clutched upon their teeth. I looked for some mothering there, and got nothing but stone.

Clinton stood by where they laid the wood, tenting a piece just so here and there. I stared until he looked up, but there was nothing in his face for me, so I stayed away. Kayla waved to me but then dropped her eyes away. Even Melda McConaughey was there. She wore a plush pink coat that looked like it could hardly be warm enough. But she passed the wood up from the trucks just like the rest of everyone.

They knew what to do without speaking. Once they had got the wood laid, Shauna went along with a stack of newspapers in one arm, crumpling paper in her other hand and stuffing it in where it could light and catch. Have you never seen a row of men go down to the earth on their sides and kiss and kiss at the air, and it was dark by then but their faces began to bloom orange as each flame caught. People, when they passed her, touched Bernadette at a place in the middle of her back. Not long, but often. She had folded her arms upon herself and pressed a clump of tissue against her face.

I was useless. The whole thing looked like a party someone had sucked the air out of. Mark Tedrow had turned the water troughs over to use for benches. You might as well point your feet to the fire, I suppose. Well. And might as well admit there was whiskey in the thermos Janice Creekmur passed down the line. I didn't presume to try and take any. I was too ashamed. It was for the people who were working, and I was not working. Mondo came and sat on my feet. He let me drop my hand through his fur, which was dirty and left a powder on my palm. But he eventually left me also. I could only be given so much. I left the circle of light and went back into the kitchen. It hurt too much to keep lying. I knew that whatever happened when I told the truth would hurt, too, but it didn't seem possible anything could feel worse, and so in some way, I passed through a door in the air. Some part of me picked up my feet and carried me out of my silence.

I called the police. The house was strange inside, so bright and empty around my voice. I told them about the phone call, Richard Klink, the horses, everything I could remember. I was a concerned neighbor who had dropped by and happened to overhear the phone call, I told them. I made it sound like it had just happened that day. I didn't give my name in case they realized that Virgil was my brother. As soon as I hung up, I called Alistair. I told him what I had told the police, and suggested he call them himself to confirm that I wasn't phoning in bullshit. I waited a long time for him to speak.

"Cindy Stoat. Weren't you at the house the last time I visited?"

"Yes," I said.

"You left before I could say hello. You ran out in such a hurry."

"I had to get home for Christmas." Why didn't he sound angry? It frightened me. A prickle crept up between my shoulder blades and plucked at the cords in my neck.

"Certainly. You spend quite a bit of time with Bernie, it seems."

"I didn't figure she should be alone."

"Cindy, perhaps you can tell me: Just when did Jude phone the house?"

"Two months ago. About." Really, it had been more like three. As much as I tried to pretend otherwise, I knew this exactly.

"I see." He held his breath. Or I did.

"I'm sorry," I said.

"Yes," he said. "I have no doubt of that." And he was gone.

I wanted to sleep for a long time, and considered it. But the greater part of me insisted that I watch everything else happen.

Nobody had stayed with the goats. They cried in little ways that I could hear. I can't think about it, ever. When I got close to them, someone at the fire stood and stared, maybe ready to up and remove me physically. I didn't understand that people could catch what was killing them, that it was dangerous. But I knew it was my task to watch it all. Maybe I can be forgiven some other things if you understand this. I did not go in the house all night, and I didn't speak. Bernadette came out with a .22 rifle and I watched as she shot each goat in the back of the head. The last of them were paralyzed, and their legs shook from the blasts. I watched. I watched the blood paint parts of them black. I thought my breath would shatter me. And I watched Mark Tedrow lay each goat on the tarp which he carried between himself and one of the other men. The goats slid into the fire. And I watched the women in coveralls stir the coals with a rake as the wood came apart into gray stones. I watched as they turned the wood over, over. And the smell of burned wet leather from their boots where they stood too close to the heat. But what was most terrible, and which I'll never forget, as the fire began to go in on the goats' carcasses, was how they seemed for a moment alive again. It was just the idea of a shiver, the way a hand twitches just before the phone rings. What was really the fire settling in and beginning to fuse their bones looked like breath returning. I thought Ann Richards and Panda Jane and Butter and Dirtbike might get up and walk out through the flames, and it seemed possible to me that we were all mistaken, none of the goats had died at all but each one of us people had, and we would stand around in the cold like this while in the other world they went on grazing, standing on cinder blocks. And maybe the fire wasn't a fire at all but the window where we could see into the other world, the better one. The true pure gold one. Of course we couldn't live there, it would burn us up, but we could see it in places where it sang through. It seemed possible, but then of course their joints began to crackle in the heat and the snapping fat rendered out and fell in dark drops that flared up when they hit the wood. The whole thing flared up. My face shrank in the heat, and when I looked away I saw the wild green blur I had burned on my eyes.

When the sun came up again, the faces grew more lines. I had no sense of the hours. It was the first time I had seen an unlovely morning, a morning which did not actually chase away all the night mood. The faces loomed up from their collars like to float away over the foothills. It was a bad thing, and I saw it again often. I would see it in all the murk of the world.

And when the cop car pulled up with its lights going but no siren, because of course there were no other drivers to get out of the way in the far place where we were, I thought completely that I would be arrested. If not for obstruction, then for basic wickedness and lies. Or possibly we would all be arrested for burning the animals. Surely there was something to arrest us for. Meanness of spirit and smallness of teeth, bad life, too dreamy, fat chin. Doctor Vic went to the officers. He hiked up his jeans to pull himself up into an official posture for explaining all this, but they stiff-armed him back. I was too far away to hear. They threaded through the crowd and pulled Bernadette out toward the cruiser. She was shaking her head and sweeping them away with the flats of her hands, but they placed her in the front seat and pulled away. When I got in closer, Janice Creekmur said, "They found her. She's alive." I started laughing. Not because I was happy exactly, but Janice spoke it over my head like she was looking upon a wheel of truth churning eternally in space. "Shut up," she said to me. Before the cops pulled up, I had actually forgotten all about my phone calls. I never imagined it would end so fast. They were taking Bernadette to Pittsburgh. Jude had been Life Flighted there just moments before.

I would know all about that later, but just then I had gone beyond weariness. Suddenly I found myself bad at pretending to be surprised. I couldn't make myself feel what anyone was feeling, and I had the crazy thought that they would see in me how I'd known all along and toss me into the fire, too, whole thing. Chill fell on me like a cold coat once I had walked away from where they were all watching. I couldn't go back in the house. It had gathered itself up against me like glass. Maybe I would have walked into the dark until I died. I considered it. It was romantic. But our truck, Virgil's truck, stuck out at the end of the straggling line of cars laid along the road, and the handle gave. I curled myself back in the pony seat. I must have slept.

XXI

Richard Klink had abducted Jude from a Uniontown bar where she was waiting for Gebe & Skocik to dump her fuel filter. He was a ticket taker at the Regal Valley Mall movie theater, and had been cut from his coast guard deployment as the result of a routine mental health screening. He was no relation of the boys who had put the sugar in her gas tank or the Burchinals who owned the general store where she broke down. He had business in Uniontown over a purebred poodle he was buying for his mother's seventieth birthday. The poodle's name was Racy, and Jude had sat with him at the bar because the dog was so friendly.

In the *60 Minutes* interview, Jude said: "He said he was going to drop me back at the mechanics. It was raining hard. I thought a little before I said yes. I actually thought, 'This is the kind of thing where you do it and they never see you again.' The dog was wagging its tail. It was like, how bad can it be? I don't know. That decided it for me. The worst part was when I noticed he was driving toward the highway. When he merged onto the highway, he was talking about baseball, like I wouldn't notice what he was doing. And the worst part was, I talked about baseball, too. I wanted to keep him calm. I thought if I was nice enough, I could get out of it. I hate baseball."

Other details would come later, as Richard Klink proved to be a highly voluble and engaging speaker on the matter of his own mind. He had to take her, he said, because she had a thousand-point star on her shoulders in place of a head and he had never seen anything so beautiful. He believed that the light in a person usually died away by the time they could drive a car. This was why he had divorced his wife: The starlight all fled from her mind. He had tried to prevent this decay in his own daughters to zero effect. Determined to manifest a perfect girlfriend for himself, when he saw Jude in the late-day dazzle of the dark bar, he had no doubt she was for him.

The police had no trouble finding the place. It was just as Jude had described. Richard Klink was a volunteer firefighter and first responder, which explained why she hadn't called 911. He'd told the local dispatchers that he was taking care of an elderly aunt who was a bit paranoid and easily confused, and so they should disregard any emergency calls made from his home address. Who knows if that could be true, but Jude believed it, which was enough. He had been keeping her in an upstairs room with the windows blacked out with roofing felt. The open door taunted her. It made it seem like she could just walk out if she wasn't afraid. Only at night, or when he left, he locked the room again.

During the day, they did what he called boyfriend-girlfriend activities, all oddly chaste: He liked to order complicated IKEA cabinets for them to assemble as a team. He had an artificial Christmas tree which they trimmed each day, and which he denuded each night. He never touched her, except to prop an arm around her shoulders when they watched reruns after supper. But he only fed her if she said "I love you," "You make me feel so safe," or any of the other desired phrases he had helpfully inscribed on index cards. People said she was lucky, how he didn't do the things you'd think a man would do. But I wasn't so sure.

Jude had managed just the once to get to the phone. There had been a fire in town, and Richard Klink forgot to lock her up as he rushed off to fight it. Everything about that time rang strange to her. Time itself had changed. She had a clear memory, a perfectly clear memory, of calling her mother, but later couldn't say when it had even happened. She didn't trust her own mind anymore. She said time had been just the one moment that she could see the beginning and end of. Over and over. She said it was like getting up on a balance beam over and over.

Reporters loved talking with Richard Klink because he said the most terrifying things in sensible tones more often used to give interstate directions or describe what had been had for breakfast.

"Some people, they think everything is about race these days. Not me. I look beyond. I thought her light could be made a little better with my help is all," he would say. "Some women need just the right environment to flower."

"Mr. Klink, you restrained her against her will for the better part of a year," the interviewer would say.

"I do not argue with God's will, sir. I do not always understand it, but I do not argue. I surrender myself in full degree. Anything else, you're talking cream and living skim milk. Surrender is worth any discomfort you'd care to witness."

"Discomfort?"

"Oh, yes. Oh yes. To shed this life. It is a difficult task. Most aren't up to it. Most don't have the grit. That little girl is better than you and me. I require us all to believe it."

I came to with lines of heat leaping off me and a block of ice in my throat. It felt like someone had replaced my knees with rubber balls. I vibrated at a frequency that might have made me disappear. The sky flooded down white and aching over everything. I was in my bed, my childhood bed, still in my farm clothes. My jeans tented around me and rubbed the hairs on my leg like a shimmer. I was holding close to me my doll with the broken neck.

I dragged up to the bathroom to put my mouth against the water but couldn't reach it on my stiff neck, and brought my hands full up and up to my face until the water in my stomach hurt.

Something, I guess, must have happened to me those days. I thought I would die of what had killed the goats. The fever washed over me, and I cried in the dark of my bedroom. I woke up to drink water. I burned a rut in my blankets. Something in the dark was seeing me, it was an eye on the wall which nobody else saw and I felt it burn what it knew about me all over. That I was myself, myself. Virgil sat with me. He said I was almost gone and I was lucky it was not all the way. I part wondered if he was real. He put his hand on my forehead and held me onto the earth, like I would float away if he didn't. For long silent hours and I wished he would leave, but when he did leave I cried. It was hopeless. He opened oranges by my bed and watched my eyes shine in the dark. Bunny, I missed you, he said. I missed you so much.

When I woke up again, it was spring. Blond You and Black You were choking against chains someone had strung up on a run between the porch beam and the rusted metal pole that held up the wash line. I had never seen them tied up before and it shocked me. It had made them meaner. The way they jumped at me I couldn't tell whether they even knew to be friendly, but after a moment I could see it was just that they were so excited to see me that it made them horrible.

Neither was I ready for what was inside the house. It was a sea of silver, waist height. At first it seemed like someone had left a lot of new furniture crammed in between the old things, but then I saw that it was cases of pop stacked everywhere so there was only a slight path between rooms. Hundreds of cases. It was really crazy that I had not noticed when I was sick. Shayna and Clinton threaded through them to the kitchen without thinking but I stood there trying to put a thought together so hard it kept me from walking. My mother had arranged some of the cases in a cube like an armchair, and was watching a show about shark hunting. The baby was sat on her lap, pulling at the air. She looked like she could be a supermarket display. "And here's Sleeping Beauty," she said when she saw me there.

Shayna realized I was up and leaned back through the doorway. "We're doing fajita night," she said. "You gonna eat?"

"What's with all the pop?" I asked.

"Clinton buys from people who buy them with EBT. Pays cash, but half what they're worth."

"What? Why?"

"He sells them to the Grapplerettes, and they sell them at wrestling matches. Oh, don't look like that."

"It's better money than you think," Clinton said. He was cutting up tomatoes and putting them in a little bowl to eat with dinner. I had never seen him do a helping thing. He was trying not to look up at me, but he did a little, and smiled small back into his hands.

The air of the food was a beautiful thing. I don't know how but it took over the whole house. It took over their faces, Clinton and Shayna, who were slapping at each other's knees between arguing over the best hot sauce: Crystal versus Cholula. *No contest, no contest*, Clinton said. He was jigging her in the ribs, she was laughing. And he looked happy. My mother was made small in the house. Something had changed places. Shayna was running things, and my mother seemed old. She held the baby with one arm and dabbed some sour cream on its mouth to eat. She held the baby like it was a basketball or something, very casual. Mom didn't eat much. "I'm doing a low-carb thing" was all she said about that, though nobody asked. There was a little late sun going golden in the windowpanes, and a blare of it creeping across the wall like a tremendous and large slow moth. Then Virgil kicked the back door open and dropped himself into a chair.

"Sit up," Mom said. She jogged her heel against his chair some.

"Um not hungry," he said. For a strange second, the way he crossed his arms, he looked just like I remembered when we were kids. I had never seen him drunk before. "Um not."

"I didn't ask was you hungry. I said sit straight."

"Ma, lay off. You know he's not gonna remember it," Shayna said. It was all news to me, her momming our mom.

"Virge, it'd be good to eat something, huh?" Clinton was getting up to fix him a plate. "Let's get you some of these good tacos." This was news to me, too. I had never heard Clinton fuss like an auntie.

"Um not fucking, fucking hungry! Fuck." Then Virgil stood up, kind of liquidy, and, with severe concentration, turned his chair upside down on the floor so the legs spiked up. "Nobody sits in this chair. Ever again." Somewhere outside, his truck started up with a rip and pulled out whining around the turns until the sound all died away.

And I let that moment pass like the coward I basically am.

There was nowhere to sit after dinner but the porch, so we sat on the porch and let the dogs off their chains and told them they were good dogs, good dogs, with our hands on their backs. And when it got dark, we went to bed.

I guess you'd say I was depressed. A funny thing happened to my time around then. I won't say it was my thinking. Now that Jude was home, I couldn't stop seeing what I imagined she saw while she was trapped. All that time, looking at the ticking white panels of a strange ceiling, and hearing the horses run outside. What a deadly silence it would have been. It had been such a long time, half a year. I tried to imagine Richard Klink suffering me into holding his hand and calling him sweetie, but I couldn't feel it. And sometimes I hit myself in the head or pinched my arms to try to feel it. I held my hand in the kettle steam until I couldn't. What I had done to Jude was not so terribly real when I was eating the figs and dabbling rosewater on my eyelids and *Nessun Dorma* and *no one leaves a star*. I had forgotten, I really had forgotten, for days at a time, where she was and what was happening to her.

But now I had no peace from it. My days had a hot fuse in the middle and burned up without fanfare. I made pots of tea, swept out the angles of every room, washed everything, and let the radio talk, anything to stop imagining it. Anything to stop imagining the moment the dial tone broke in when Bernadette hung up on Jude and her world shrank back down to its terrible true form. I lived inside a fever. It was wanting all hot and awful to have not done what I had done. The very world met me where I was, and it was shadow and horrible light with not a great deal of the between. I have never again been so old as I was that spring.

My mother and I moved around each other very carefully. If we stayed in the same room for too long, it felt like that part of the house would get heavy and fall down into the valley. I can't explain it.

"I'm making fried chicken tonight," she would say. "Wanna help me?" And when I didn't say anything, she edged away like a shamed dog. Shayna and Clinton started looking for an apartment in town. The baby tracked me the way I would follow the weather: watching each moment shift and tremble and mean nothing personal. I did not interact with him as he seemed maybe a little too smart. His eyes were too shining. I believed if I held him, he'd tell the truth of what went on in my mind.

Virgil stayed drunk, with little variation. Apparently his cell mate had been the artisan pruno brewer of SCI Greene, and that was how he found his first drunk, how he found his first real magic. And since then you couldn't say a thing about shouldn't he slow down or eat something or shut the fuck up. He had been wrongfully imprisoned and had honed the edge of that bad luck so you couldn't say a word without him cutting you back down. One day, I talked him into going to Heaven Lake, just for a memory. But he couldn't get up over the fence, and cut his hand open on a loose wire, and so much blood swam out of him that I thought he would die before we got back to the house. The bottle in his back pocket busted when he hit the ground, and he was furious with me (*you bitch, you bitch*) for the whole miserable idea. A lake! What is a lake going to do? Is a lake going to live my life for me, Cindy? Get this bullshit off of me.

I thought I was living in a bag of air and what was real was in the bag with me, and there was nothing in the bag. We sat on the porch and watched the wind stir the trees. Winter hardly had any teeth left in it, just the early dark and the pink flags of the sky.

XXII

Just when the night was beginning to lose its full dark, just when the gray edges of things began to surface in my room, I heard the truck idling in the road, luffing and settling like a grouse.

The farmer had a brown coat and a T-shirt underneath it and suspenders held his jeans up over his hard, round stomach. His tits sloped off him in triangles where they met his belly, and he wore thick bifocals attached to his head with an elastic band. In the dark, they winked at me. I had gone through the waist-high sea of silver pop cans to answer the door.

"Virgil in?"

"Of course," I said. The clipboard man from the school had been coming around, getting me enrolled to repeat the ninth grade, so I was completely relieved this man had nothing to do with all that. "What is this about?"

"He's driving. Got to take this grip out to Milwaukee."

"What!" I had no idea what a grip was, but I figured it out immediately.

"I'll wait here." He stayed outside, stepping from shoe to shoe as if it were cold. A young boy, but pale, sat up in the passenger side of the truck and looked at me hard with the hating way you do when you're sleepy. He was kindergarten age. His hair was cut by hand, I could tell. The edge was jagged like teeth and some of it stuck up in the back, like a splinter of wood was coming out of his head.

In Virgil's room, I couldn't see because the alarm clock was too bright. It threw the rest of the space into a harder darkness. I shook him, then pinched his nose. He was fully passed out drunk still. My brother's eyes were like white glass, with some blue threaded in them. He looked for a second as if he had gone blind. He was trying to realize who I was.

"Cindy," he said. "You got to go back to bed."

"There's a man here with some, I think, drugs for you? You probably better get up."

"Hup, hup, no," he said. "He's supposed to not come around until later."

"He's here now, I promise for real," I said.

"No."

"Fine, I'll talk to him."

I went to the kitchen and made coffee. The farmer had turned off his truck. He had the boy on the porch with him. They sat side by side on the swing, barely moving to keep the chains from squeaking.

"This is Grady," he said, laying his heavy hand down on the boy's head. "He got himself a little bit of a fever."

"You should come in. There's coffee inside."

"Whyn't you sit up out here with Grady."

I didn't want to, but he pulled me down and sat me. He went into the house, where Virgil had turned on a light in the kitchen. I saw a wedge of it coming from down the hall.

The boy leaned against me and put his arm around my waist.

"Ew, no," I said.

The skin on his arms was hot. He smelled like a swimming pool, like bleach and sunscreen and zinc. He almost glowed. But then of course I realized the light was coming up all around us. And then he was blue, and he looked like he was sitting there in the light of a dark planet.

I had gotten the idea from somewhere that you were supposed to sing to a child with a fever. So I sang a song for Grady. My voice was harsh because I was trying to keep it quiet. I made up something about a boat at the bottom of the ocean, where the fish were just bones and the moon never saw. It was silly and poetic. I hated it but I felt the swish of it burning up my arms and my eyes and the place where my tongue rooted into my mouth. Our feet whisked over the bare dust of the porch and the talking inside got tenser. I imagined it like a tight string, a string pulled tight between my brother and the farmer. They both held the string in their teeth. And took turns plucking it, one or the other of them.

My throat hurt. I wondered if Grady's fever had leaped onto my skin. The light hurt my eyes. It was getting to be day.

The farmer came outside and loped over to his truck. He was moving fast, but leaning sideways, and I realized he was extremely drunk. A red light went on over his head, like an oven timer. Sometimes I saw things like that.

He threw two trash bags on the apron of yard that wound around the forsythia bushes and started the truck going down the road before he remembered his son. He dashed back to us there and picked Grady up by the armpits. Grady's legs swung wide and one of his miniature cowboy boots smacked me on the bridge of the nose. The farmer carried him up high like a king.

Virgil had a hand over his left eye at the kitchen table. He was wearing sweatpants and his hair had a shine on it. He looked like a statue somebody had just unloaded and left there.

One of the trash bags was full of little black bricks in plastic wrapping. Somebody had put it in with a bunch of clothes still on the hangers, thick pink shirts with hibiscus flowers sewed on around the neck holes, white shirts with blue threads ticked in them, and like the things elderly teachers wore. The other was all money, individual bills. They were dirty feeling, slick with being touched too much. But they smelled like money, of course. I had not seen that much money all at once. It was a new feeling. I put my head in the bag and breathed for a while. I wanted to show Grady, then recalled he had already been taken. Virgil began strapping the bricks down in a layer under Wade's baby carrier, and then he sat up at the kitchen table cutting a pocket in the clean diapers with a razor blade, shoving the bundles inside. It seemed just nutso to me. It didn't seem like an especially inconspicuous way to travel, a man alone with lots of diapers and no baby. I guess he thought babies just canceled everything out, even suspicion and bad acts. I went back to sleep, and when I woke up, all the stuff was cleared out. My brother was gone.

XXIII

Hardly three months after the goats and the fire and my disappearing brother, I washed up again on the shores of West Greene High School, where in the mornings, the classroom TVs played a three-minute clip of an American flag waving in a blue sky, which we were supposed to adore. The halls had a hectic, soupy feel I didn't remember. My heart froze every time someone talked to me. I hadn't talked to anyone my age all year. I forgot what you do. I felt like my words were made out of bones and hot dogs and nonsense. Maybe I could just do charades all year. I was trying to do the charades of INVISIBLE. I had home ec first period. I didn't know anyone in my classes that well since I had been held back. The girls in my new class liked to flip through the Butterick sewing pattern catalog to pick out and name their future husbands and children. I was horrified. Maybe my year with Bernadette had turned me into a snob. But I was horrified all the same.

Clinton and Shayna moved into town, half an hour away, and Virgil never came back, so it was Mom and Wade and me only. Mom went back to work at the hospital. Most of the time she left Wade with Shayna, but sometimes I would get off the school bus and find him crying in the kitchen, with the house empty except for a few squares of twilight roaming the walls. Every time, I thought it was happening all over again. I would ditch my homework and mash up Hamburger Helper for Wade and sing to him about how we had been abandoned to die in the woods, and the grass would eat us up and whisper our names. I don't know, but it didn't feel so serious when I sang, even though I knew I was singing to fool myself. But then Mom would get home around midnight with a bucket of fried chicken and act like it was normal, and in fact not say anything about how late she was. I liked Wade more and more. When she held him, he'd turn bright red.

School had been OK before, but when I went back, I started picking up detentions. I wasn't trying to be funny. I had gotten used to adults talking normally to me, and forgot that teachers didn't care for us to be friends. In Western civ, Mr. Mulgrove would call on me to describe the extent of the Roman Empire, and I'd say wasn't democracy basically Roman? Only he'd interrupt me: "I mean on the *map*, Miss Stoat." Everybody laughed. But wasn't I answering a more interesting question? My teachers didn't care.

Most days I played a game. In the game, I was a Soviet gymnast, single-minded and misunderstood, staring into the middle distance on the school bus, in home ec, or wherever. I had been brought here by mistake. I didn't speak the language or understand the customs, but it was nevertheless my job to make my way. My life was a movie about this. The people I imagined watching the movie sympathized with me, but all the other characters—my mother, Mr. Mulgrove, every boy who muttered "fish" when I walked past their seat on the school bus—had no idea how stupid they looked.

A normal teenage life, in other words.

But then the story came out in *People* magazine. "BIZARRE KIDNAPPING MYSTERY! An 18-year-old's cries for help unheard? What new forensic evidence may reveal, inside," it said. They had shot the cover on Bernadette's porch. Jude wore a bomber jacket and tall boots, with one hand on Mondo's back as if she could sic him with a gesture. In the background, hanging in the window, I recognized a string of garlics Bernadette and I had braided together to dry the day before all the goats got sick. I had not allowed myself to miss her at all before then.

At the worst, I had not considered the possibility of an exposé. Apparently, there was a message board where armchair detectives drilled down phone logs and public records, particularly in strange cases like Jude's, and someone who knew Clinton put the pieces together. *People* had interviewed Alistair, Doctor Vic, and even Clinton to establish that I had been living at Bernadette's house while Jude was missing. A timeline crawled the spread, nailing down when I had lived there, when Jude disappeared, and, thanks to phone records, when Jude had called the house for help. Some psych doctor described Bernadette's mental state as "histrionic and quite suggestible," hinting that she might have been induced to believe her daughter was not missing, thus taking the tip less seriously than she might otherwise. And, of course, in the sidebar they ran my seventh-grade school picture. My hair was dark with grease. I wore a stained pink sweatshirt and a vending machine angel pendant on a piece of green string. I had smiled in the picture, but it didn't come from my eyes. If I didn't know myself, I would believe that girl could do something terrible.

The article didn't necessarily conclude anything or accuse me, but it wasn't hard to see what they were putting together. They interviewed teachers and kids from school, too. "I always knew something was off," and "It's no wonder, with her family." The same psych doctor said: "Unvented childhood trauma can have disastrous consequences. Sometimes, in prolonged suffering, children break from reality. This is called psychosis." I, of course, had not been reached for comment. This didn't surprise me since I had been trying my best to avoid mail and telephones. The sidebar noted other victim frauds, like the mom in Orange County who beat herself with chains and accused four invented black men of kidnapping her, and the Swiss writer who invented a childhood at Auschwitz even though he was born too late to live it. I tried to imagine being a mom in California who thought she needed to be beaten to let her sadness exist. In the picture, she was standing in the nosebleeds at a football stadium, perfect blond hair like honey through a prism. Her life didn't look like a problem. These were people where the middle part of them had been rotted and eaten by something that never saw the daylight. Whatever was in them stayed hidden and got muscles. And once it had muscles, it did all the talking. I saw it. Hello, myself, I said.

When they asked Jude about me, she said: “I don’t know. I used to go out with her brother. She was a sneaky kid. Once, she watched us kissing. That was weird. She was so little. She just stood there. It gave me the creeps.”

“Do you forgive her?” they asked Jude.

“Wouldn’t it be awfully spiritual if I could say yes?” she said.

I would have liked to go to jail. I actually called the police and confessed. They put Detective Torboli on the phone. Apparently he was working a double homicide, and found me annoying. I mean, he thought I was crazy. “Honey, everybody’s alive. That’s pretty good, trust me. Why don’t you just get on with it?” But he didn’t understand: I didn’t know how to. All the rest of that year, I couldn’t make any of my old ideas work about why what I did was OK. It had seemed like such an important distinction, that I hadn’t personally kidnapped anybody. The interviewer also asked Jude how she was adjusting to life at home.

“I hear horses. I hear them running. I could hear them in the room where he kept me. It’s just a sound in the background. Everywhere I go.” My breath would grab at me and stick in my guts when I thought about it, so I did what I had to do to hold my thumb over the sun of it.

I used food, mostly. I ate to disappear. I ate to float. I had learned this a long time before. It felt like the rock I was born on, the most home of my homes. Trauma? My life didn’t seem exactly as serious as that, but I really didn’t know anymore. The funny thing was: Exactly nobody talked to me about the article. I saw people passing it around in the cafeteria. Sometimes I heard people calling me trauma girl, trash girl.

It got quiet whenever I passed through a room. I went everywhere in a tide of silence.

I didn't call it praying. I didn't call it anything. And it wasn't to god, because nobody in my family knew what that was about.

I learned how to do it in winter, when the snow was flying. I went to the window and saw it soft with my eyes. I saw it all at once. In the edges of the snow and places between were the hills, and hills of sticks poured around them. Smoke came up from farther off in Deep Valley, and also smoke from Bernadette's house below, where the gray was blown up with blue for a minute before pure dark. I could see the lines very clearly, between branches and sky, and lines in the sky from jets that never thought about us. In between all the snow was edges and edges and edges, which I felt myself pulled into. It was a quiet room in there. My blood was the sound of it.

Something talked to me in the room. The words were plain and I also didn't know where they came from. They were answers to questions that I had not asked: Go walk. See that can in the mud? Pick it up and throw it away. Look at the space between the snow. Look a second time. The baby needs a new diaper. There is a part of you that will always live outside your body, in the stars. You don't have to keep doing this to yourself. Be still. You have never been alone. Wash the dishes for your mother. Sweep the porch out for yourself. Anything you make nice for someone else is made good for you, too. Hold the baby. Hold him. Hold him. There. Be still and let yourself feel it. You are a glory, forever and ever.

I started taking long walks and picking up trash on the road. I appreciated the feeling of it, and kept going. I washed the floor in the kitchen, and polished the windows with vinegar and newspaper. I told Sissy Pecjak about all the things I stole, and she let me work off the debt after school. A strange thing was happening. Another world bloomed up inside my old one. It wasn't that anything got better, necessarily. People still whispered about the magazine article, and I still swarmed with shame whenever I ran into Jude or saw her splitting wood when the school bus went by. School was brutal. My mother cut off the hair I had dyed black, so I had a fluffy mullet look, halfway between a teenager and a forty-something bank teller. But I felt the air on my neck in a way that seemed light and unusual. I don't know how to describe it. I didn't fight the fact of what I had done. It was true, and also I could pick up trash on the road and hold my brother. It sounds so small to say it like that, but it lent my life a little motion.

Sometimes I wrote letters to Virgil. I traced them with my finger on my school desk or the marble pebble school-bus seat, or into the cave of my hand. *H-E-Y-V-I-R-G-I-L. G-U-E-S-S-W-H-A-T. M-O-M-I-S-B-E-I-N-G-W-E-I-R-D-A-B-O-U-T-T-H-E-L-O-T-T-E-R-Y-A-G-A-I-N.* And also *I-L-O-V-E-Y-O-U-I-M-I-S-S-Y-O-U-I-M-S-O-R-R-Y.*

March came in with a last big snow. Mom and Wade stayed over in town when the roads got bad, and I stayed in bed until my throat itched. School would be canceled for two days. The house was pale inside from all the scrawny snow light, and exploded with ladybugs. I was excited because I had a new book from the library and I was going to be alone with it at last, so I arranged for maximum pleasure a jar of peanut butter and sleeve of saltines so I could eat and float and read all at once, my favorite combination.

But as soon as I pulled my chair up to the furnace, the voice said: Go dig out the driveway for Jude.

I disregarded. The snow was eight inches at least. There was no reason to trifle with it. Someone else probably dug out their driveway anyway. They probably didn't need to go anywhere. Jude probably liked the excuse to get outside. The snow wasn't that deep, anyway. They had an all-wheel drive truck and everything was supposed to melt by the end of the week. And what if she saw me? What if she chased me off? What if she called the police?

Get up. Go dig out the driveway for Jude. Get up. Get up.

I got back into bed and hoped that moving would shake the voice off of me. I was starting to sweat. I moved my eyes over the book but they didn't land anywhere. I'm cold, I thought. I'm trash girl. My life is hard and I deserve a break. School is hard. I deserve a break. I need it. The voice went silent in response, which scared me. I peeled off the blankets and shook furiously as I shrugged into Virgil's old lined barn jacket.

It was actually sort of warm outside. It was one of those days when the snow feels like cotton all around you. No wind. And as I stomped down through the woods to Bernadette's house, I rehearsed all the things that Jude might yell at me. It seemed like it would help, to rehearse them, although it only made the moment that I walked up to the drive and pushed my first shovel of snow seem like a showdown, loud in the drama of my heart. Nothing happened, of course. I kept working. After a while, my back got tight, so I knew I was doing an OK job. My breath turned flinty and wet in my scarf, and once I hit a rhythm, I didn't look up or much think outside the way I was breathing. I started at the road and moved in, feeling the muscles in my forearms burn and pull. I love work. Work like that has sometimes been my only peace.

It wasn't until I got near the house that I saw Jude. She was standing on the porch in a big blank sweatshirt ashing a Camel into a coffee mug, with a little shiver bouncing her leg. She wasn't dressed for outside but it looked like she had been waiting there a minute. We looked at each other for a long time. I felt like this had all happened before. It was like the day I saw her kissing Virgil. Time flowed out, and I wavered in its center. I couldn't shake the echo. Some part of me got lost halfway out of my body. I don't know. No part of me moved.

I waved hi.

A long second later, she waved hi also.

I finished the end of the drive and leaned the shovel where I had found it, and went back up into the woods without looking behind.

Jude ended up doing a few semesters at Carnegie Mellon, but she dropped out to take care of Bernadette. She got her mom through a hospital detox, but it had an unintended effect: The prior news about Jude's disappearance seemed to finally sink in. Bernadette would call the state troopers, hissing *Someone knows where she is, you bastards*, all the more devastating because it was true. They did know, and they told her—and then she called again ten minutes later. When Jude hid the phones, it only made Bernadette more certain that the fix was in. She set off in the woods searching and cried in the tub, even though Jude was long since found. She was sure a KGB spy traced her from the hills with binoculars, so she decided to smoke the bastard out, only to kill one of the Creekmurs' cows. She set out traps on the road with carpet tacks—the postmaster was just about done with her. They even moved her into assisted living in Cranberry, but Bernadette had hotwired a limo and crashed a retired Steelers defensive back's annual holiday party, so no more of that. These dramas were impeccably timed to scuttle Jude's midterms or finals.

Once Alistair got power of attorney, he hired live-in care for Bernadette. It was no trouble to afford such a thing, but entirely another to keep someone in the position. The nurses generally lasted about two months. Many of them, I'm sure, were not ready for the isolation, how the house could go spooky on you in the night, and how your cell phone wouldn't work unless you drove to the top of Centennial Hill, in the graveyard. But also, Bernadette, in certain moods, anointed the house with her urine. She laid hexes on her caretakers by writing their names on slips of paper and freezing them in the ice cube tray. One nurse she had successfully poisoned with laurel roots. She still whipped herself in moments of emotion. It was too much.

Jude was still just about the only black person in that part of the county. She was conspicuous before, but after the kidnapping, people somehow got the idea she was magic, since she had survived such a terrible thing. Ruthie Rush tried to clip a chunk of hair from the back of Jude's head when she was waiting in line at the feed store. Some of the lesser Creekmurs dug through her trash for tokens or sigils. They brought their sick babies and busted knees and glaucomas around for her to somehow heal. For could she not remove the hurts from the body? And could she not tell them something about living in the terrible lasting moments that would break your heart? And wasn't she pure, since evil had not burned her away, and wouldn't the pure one hold the hurt forever? Well. Jude eventually brought out the shotgun to shoo them off her land, and just to hell with it. She had another idea for herself. And that is where I came, again, into her life.

She called at the house during *Wheel of Fortune*, which Wade and I enjoyed best. We liked the things people guessed when there weren't enough hint letters, or when they were too dim to take the hint. They always said something that gave away their inner mind: "HELL SHINE HARDER!" "I PUSH THE PILLS FOR DREAMY!" "DONKY PUNKY!" It was the last week of school, and a little more than a year since Jude was found and brought home. The air had more space in it than usual. More warm motion was shining over the hills.

"Could I speak with Cindy?" she said when I picked up the phone.

"This is Cindy."

"Huh. You know, we really do sound alike."

"Who is this?"

"It's Jude. I was hoping you could come down before dinner. There's something I wanted to bring up."

"OK. Wow. Yeah."

"Just to be clear. I don't want to hear any 'sorry.' We're not doing that. You have to take that somewhere else. Do you understand?" I didn't, but I didn't say anything.

"Oh. OK. I won't. Should I—"

"Come by at five," she said, and hung up. I put on a blouse for some reason. I had started dressing up whenever I didn't understand what was going on. It seemed like Jude had requested my appearance in a private court, and I went with my head heavy down the hill in the lufting spring twilight. The spring peepers had just started singing maybe the week before, and all around me a blue light washed the rocks and small new leaves. My breath went all the way through my body, very solid, the way it would sometimes after I had been crying.

The house gleamed like a ship. It had been a few months since I had come down to shovel. It looked like a brand-new thing. Someone had set it to right. Someone had put up a smart-looking split-rail fence behind the barn, and a glossy red porch swing inched on the breeze. There were again goats in the pen. Not amber grays like the Kiko-Alpines. I didn't know what they were. They didn't know what I was either. Heat sang up from the grass. My stomach looped.

Jude was at the door. "Well, come on," she said.

I was dizzy to be inside the house again. There were still shabby spots along the baseboards and all the crowded ideograms and amulets hung in their secret configurations, but the junk was all gone and everything looked like it had been swept and set and made right and kept up in a way that made the room feel cool and light. Bernadette was nowhere. The barn kitten was now a sluggish yellow tom that spotted me over its shoulder and declared me uncompelling. I followed Jude to the kitchen, where she flatted her hands on the table like a teacher who's about to tell you that you failed a test.

"So," Jude said. "They've sent you to therapy, huh?"

I had no idea how she knew this.

"I saw you a few times. My therapist is in the same building." When she saw the look on my face, she said, "Relax, it isn't the same one. That would be fucked up though, wouldn't it?" She seemed amused by this. Without especially paying attention to her hands, she got up and began chopping dill into green dust. Something about it reminded me exactly of Bernadette. "I wonder if that ever happens. In the morning, you hear 'He done me wrong,' and in the afternoon, you hear the opposite. Shoot, I bet some therapists are kind of into it. Small-town soap opera." I must have looked horrified, because she came back to the table with a bowl of dip and crackers. Rabbits and moons and stars around the rim—Alistair's gift. "It's beet hummus. I know, I know. But Mom likes it. She calls it dippable borscht."

I took a cracker up to my mouth and chewed and nodded without tasting anything.

"You can talk, you know."

I swallowed hard. "I don't know where to start. I really don't know what to say."

"When I don't know what to say, I usually ask a question."

"How are you doing? Since you've been back?"

"Ha!" And like Bernadette, she also threw back her head when she laughed. "Tricky question! I don't ever answer it, myself. Try again."

"What did you want to talk about?"

"Fair enough. I have a proposal for you. For now, I just want you to listen to it. Don't decide."

"OK."

"Well—you probably heard about Mom. She's worse, actually. I mean, she's been sober since last July, and her vitals are great. But her memory has gotten way worse. She's more confused."

"I heard about the cow."

"Yeah, that. She's been getting a little dangerous, I hate to say. Not for me, but people she doesn't know, she doesn't trust them. She's sure everybody's part of some big lie." A spike of ice fell through me. I had never imagined this consequence to my pretending. "And it's dangerous for her, too. She can't be here alone. One day I forgot to lock up the medicine cabinet and she OD'd on fish oil capsules because she kept thinking she had forgotten to take them. No big deal, she just felt sick. But something worse would happen eventually."

"You want to leave."

"Are you for real? Of course I want to leave. I've been trying to get out of here since I was six. But also, I got into Yale for religious studies. I want to go. And I don't want to be back here every weekend because Mom poisoned the UPS guy again, you know?"

"Religious studies? You don't seem like, I don't know—"

"Ethics," she said, and cut her eyes up to mine, almost smiling. "Anyway, I guess I'm trying to ask if you'll live with her again."

"Full time?"

"Around the clock. I mean, you know what she's like. She can get into a lot of trouble in a few hours, but if you sit around with her, she just drinks her tea and tells you stories about the Hapsburgs."

"What about school?"

"I wondered about, well, I guess I thought you might drop out, like Clinton did? We'd be paying you out of the settlement, I guess. I didn't know how much school mattered to you. Dad and I haven't talked about it, but I bet he would help you get in a GED program."

"Paying me?"

"Minimum wage! I don't know. This is all Dad's idea, honestly. But, yeah, it's work. You know how it is. I know you do. She isn't easy. Really, don't say anything now. Think on it overnight, take a week, whatever you need. It's asking a lot. I don't want you to say you can do it just because you feel obligated."

"I am obligated."

"Well. I don't know what you think. You should just take your time, that's what I'm saying."

I couldn't put my mind to what was strange, exactly. I had imagined falling to my knees, Jude wailing or speaking from a quiet wrath. I don't know. She had tucked her feet up under her and sent the pom-pom on her hoodie tumbling back and forth across her chest in a distracted and easy fashion. Her head came to a bit of a tilt when she looked up, considering her words as she said them, as if she was watching them float away in bubbles.

"Do you ever hear from Virgil?" she asked me.

"No. Not really. He used to send me postcards."

"Me either. Not lately, anyway. He used to call me in the middle of the night. To talk about spaghetti, baseball, weird stuff like that. I just hoped he'd make his way back here eventually."

"Me, too. He might. Who knows." A little blue tint was sneaking into the light. The tears came up in my eyes but didn't spill over until I blinked. "Can I ask you something? I don't know if it's OK to ask."

"Go for it."

"Why are you doing this?"

"Well, not for your sake. I'll tell you that much."

"Huh?"

"Oh, Cindy. I don't intend to waste my life on you," she said. "That's all."

Well. No one leaves a star, like they say.

It's not like it was, but then, I wasn't really taking care of Bernadette before. Oh, I made her pots of tea and kept up the goats and washed the dishes, and it all seemed so adult at the time. Never mind how I fed her all this gin. Stone sober, I sometimes catch Bernadette stomping a bat she caught in a shoebox. She's still seeing William Holden movies in reflective surfaces, but this no longer disturbs me. In fact, it makes her easier to corral, as I have no more of my old tricks. Jude made it entirely clear that I am to be myself only and always, and I respect that wish, even though I sometimes wake up in the night to find Bernadette at the foot of my bed, demanding to know this second who I am, holding out her favorite quartz spike to impel me. Once, she wedged a pile of poison sumac leaves into my pillow, and my lip swelled up so big it hung off my face. She is, I think, really trying to kill me sometimes. Anytime I've left my dinner unattended, I chuck it out the back door into the garden, just in case.

Before, I never thought once about Bernadette's vitamins, medicine, sleeping, cholesterol. I am now quite rigorous on those matters. I bathe her feet. I lotion her cankers. I check her blood sugar. We bicker about whether we've already eaten our half baked potato and our scoop of cottage cheese like old married sad-o types, and I love it. Some nights Shayna comes down to spell me a few hours, and I drive into town, just to slap my eyes upon a stranger and see some neon lights. When Jude and Alistair visit, I stay with my mom, and we do what we can to be together. It's not much, although we both like cleaning. We're repainting the house room by room.

The goats I don't name. That is my truce with them. I change their hay perfectly. Sometimes, when I milk them, though, I lay my forehead against the shuddering warm cages of their ribs, and cry.

I did negotiate one term: I asked to bring Wade. Jude didn't like it, considering, I suppose, how easy he would be to poison. But she figured it was my problem, and why not. Thank god. Bernadette has no idea who he is, except in the way that all children belong to a divinity which she has never ceased answering to. The goblin prince, the babe o' the bower. Little junco, shuggie bear, *schatzilein*. She's made a million names for him. She'd cut a wedge out of the sun if it would please him.

"You will grow up to be a king," she tells Wade. I almost believe it. She's teaching him all the bones in the body, all the birds and flowers and beetles. And how to sing "La Bamba." I don't know what we'll do when he goes to kindergarten. We'll have to take up goat soap operas again, I suppose.

Jude said she didn't intend to waste her life on me, and I was hurt. I didn't know what she meant. But now I think: I don't intend to waste my life on me either. Not on my mother, not on Clinton, not on myself, not on the flames of old hurt. I do not care to stand in the doorway of myself, making a list of punishments. I'm the kind who can only see the road ahead so far. I'm the kind that has to get empty somehow. I tried all the other ways. The only one that wouldn't kill me was taking care of friends and wildlife. I'm no martyr, I promise. No savior, no hero, no saint—I eat too many figs to qualify, I'm afraid. Neither do I think some tally will be balanced. I'm not sure I can be forgiven in full.

But on some mornings, the air is washed in an old way I remember, and Bernadette says:

"Ann Richards, I am getting sick to death of you stealing my black beaded sweater."

"Is that right?" I say.

"Oh yes, I am heavy tired of it. I know you sold it for one thin dime."

In a place where the air was ancient. "Why, yes. Redondo Beach," I tell her. "I'm a teenage runaway. You'll never take me alive!" This is our best homemade joke. We tell it to each other all day.

And then I read her Jude's letters, or I read to her from the 1977 *Fern Finder*, her favorite book. "If blade is strap-like with a blunt tip and oblique sori, it is Hart's-Tongue." "Spore-bearing parts: See next page (important)." And on like that, and on like that, in the chilly blue world without boredom. Wade introduces us to the monsters of the earth and sea, all quite personal to him. He runs with the goblins of the forest. We make lemon curd for the postmaster and mend pants with those awful waxy patches and notice the new smells in the air. I move my hands over what needs done, and I get empty, I get gone.

I'm a throat.

It's a song.

ACKNOWLEDGMENTS

This book is dedicated to Janice Hatfield, my eighth grade English teacher and the first person who told me that I could be a writer. I don't know where else I'd be, Mrs. H.

Thanks to my parents, Dan and Jan Smith. Thanks to all the families that sustain me.

Thank you to all the teachers, staff, and students at the Michener Center for Writers and the Iowa Writers' Workshop, in particular Antonya Nelson, Colm Toibin, Charlie Baxter, Ethan Canin, Sam Chang, and Daniel Orozco. Special thanks to Marla Akin, Deb West, Jan Zenisek, and Connie Brothers. Thanks also to the MacDowell Colony and the Rona Jaffe Wallace Foundation.

Thank you Atom Atkinson, Lillian-Yvonne Bertram, Anne Marie Rooney, Ben Pelhan, Zach Harris, Scott Andrew, Ethen Jerrett, Greg Koehler, Smith Henderson, Martha Stallman, Tony Tulathimutte, Meredith Blankenship, Ben Watson, Nana Nkweti, Kyle Minor, Nicole Boss, Corinne Beaugard, Brian Booker, Jake Hooker, Garth Greenwell, William Wingo, Tracy Towley, Charlie Verploegh, Anna Rauhoff, Michael Glaviano, Haley Butera, Jess Williams, Clara Wilch, Robin Bower, Jason Kirker, Bri Cavallero, and James Yu for help of every possible kind. To the entire May Day Marching Band, my total gratitude. To my beloved cat, Nellie Belle, thank you especially.

Thank you forever to everyone at Riverhead Books and Hamish Hamilton. Claudia Ballard, thank you for reading so damn many drafts of this book. And Sarah McGrath, thank you for showing me its truest and best shape.